As Chivalrous As A Fairy-Tale Paladin...

He slipped off his tuxedo jacket and draped it over her shoulders.

"You don't have to do that," Della protested. The garment fairly swallowed her, but it was redolent with both his scent and his warmth, and she was helpless not to pull it more closely around herself.

"Now you'll get cold," she told him.

Marcus shook his head. "I haven't been cold since the moment I laid eyes on you. A little thing like snow and a subfreezing temperature isn't going to change that."

Della wasn't feeling cold, either. Not that that would make her return his jacket to him. It felt too nice being enveloped in it. Almost as if she were being enveloped by Marcus himself.

Almost.

Dear Reader,

It's time for another visit to Talk of the Town, Chicago's most famous haute couture rental boutique. (All right, *my* most famous haute couture rental boutique. In fact, my only haute couture rental boutique.) This time around, it's Della Hannan who's looking to spiff herself up, and for a very special occasion. See, Della made a promise to herself when she was a kid, that for her thirtieth birthday, she'd celebrate in major style. She also promised herself as a kid that she'd be a millionaire by the time she turned thirty, but we can't have everything, can we?

So even if the millionaire thing will be pretend, the style will be quite real—even if it is rented.

The only problem is, Della can't afford to be noticed out and about because she has a little secret. Okay, okay, a *huge* secret. But it's hard to go unnoticed when one is arrayed from head to toe in the likes of Carolina Herrera and Dolce & Gabbana. And notice her Marcus Fallon does. Big-time. The last thing that guy wants to do, however, is be kept a secret. Go big or go home, that's Marcus. But when he and Della get snowed in for a weekend, he doesn't want her to go anywhere…

I hope you have as much fun reading about Della and Marcus as I had writing them. And may all your dreams be stylish ones.

Happy reading!

Elizabeth Bevarly

Caught in the Billionaire's Embrace

ELIZABETH BEVARLY

MILLS & BOON®

All the characters in this book have no existence outside
the imagination of the author, and have no relation
whatsoever to anyone bearing the same name or names.
They are not even distantly inspired by any individual
known or unknown to the author, and all the incidents
are pure invention.

First published in Great Britain 2012
by Mills & Boon, an imprint of Harlequin (UK) Limited.
Large Print edition 2012
Harlequin (UK) Limited,
Eton House, 18-24 Paradise Road,
Richmond, Surrey TW9 1SR

© Elizabeth Bevarly 2011

ISBN: 978 0 263 22964 6

Harlequin (UK) policy is to use papers that are natural,
renewable and recyclable products and made from
wood grown in sustainable forests. The logging
and manufacturing process conform to the legal
environmental regulations of the country of origin.

Printed and bound in Great Britain
by CPI Antony Rowe, Chippenham, Wiltshire

ELIZABETH BEVARLY

is the RITA® Award-nominated, nationally bestselling author of more than five dozen books. When she's not writing, she's watching *Project Runway* and *What Not to Wear*, but only for research purposes. She's also confident that she'll someday find a story in *House Hunters International*, so she watches that religiously, too. In the meantime, she makes do with her real life of ready-to-wear from Macy's and college exploratory trips around the Midwest with her husband and soon-to-be-a-senior son.

For everyone who's ever worked in women's fashion, especially employees of The Limited stores in Cherry Hill and Echelon Malls, where I got my start in writing by penning pages in the stockroom during lunch. I miss you guys. A lot.

One

There was only one thing that could make Della Hannan's thirtieth birthday better than she'd already planned for it to be, and it was a thing she hadn't even planned. That was saying something, since she'd been fine-tuning the details for the celebration since she was a little girl growing up in the kind of neighborhood where birthdays were pretty much unaffordable and therefore pretty much ignored. Where a lot of things were unaffordable and therefore ignored. Things like, well…Della, for instance. But that was why she had promised herself such a festive event. Because, even as a little girl, she'd known she had only herself to count on.

Of course, the past eleven months had rather thrown a wrench in that line of thinking, because since meeting Geoffrey, she'd had no choice but to count on him. Geoffrey wasn't here tonight, though, and she wasn't going to let herself think about him or anything else from that world. Tonight was special. Tonight was for her. And it would be everything an underprivileged kid from one of New York's roughest neighborhoods could have imagined.

Back then, Della had sworn that by the time she turned thirty, she would have escaped the mean streets of her borough and become a self-made millionaire living park-side uptown. And she'd vowed to mark the big three-oh in the style of the rich and famous, that she had imagined she'd become accustomed as this point in life. She wasn't about to renege on that promise, even if she was celebrating in Chicago instead of New York. She would begin with dinner at a five-star restaurant, follow that with a box seat at the opera and top it off with a nightcap at the sort of club that allowed entrée to only the crème de la crème of society. She was outfitted in thousands of dollars worth of haute couture, dripping in rubies and diamonds, and she had been coiffed and manicured at the city's finest salon.

She sighed with much contentment as she enjoyed the first part of her evening. Palumbo's on State Street was the sort of restaurant where prices rivaled the budgets of some sovereign nations. She had, it went without saying, ordered the most expensive items on the menu—four courses, all of which bore European names she'd had to practice all week to pronounce correctly. (Thank goodness the menu had been posted online so she could check in advance and not appear as some kind of philistine when she ordered. And how lovely to have the opportunity to use the word *philistine,* even if it was only in her head.) Because ordering the most expensive items on one's birthday was what anyone who was sophisticated and chic and rich would do, right?

The thought made her surreptitiously survey her surroundings, to make sure the other diners—sophisticated, chic and rich, every last one of them—were also enjoying the most expensive bounty. And, okay, okay, to also make sure Geoffrey hadn't somehow followed her, even though she'd done an excellent job sneaking out—she always did—and even though she wasn't scheduled to check in with him until her daily call tomorrow. He couldn't know where she was going, anyway, even if he did discover she'd slipped out when she wasn't supposed to. She'd planned tonight's escape even more meticulously than she'd planned her thirtieth birthday celebration.

For all anyone here knew, she was just as blue-blooded as they were and belonged in this society every bit as much. And, thankfully, there was no sign of Geoffrey anywhere. Check and check.

And Della did feel as if she belonged here, sipping champagne as she anticipated the arrival of her calamari appetizer. She'd been moving in environments like this for years, despite not having been born into a wealthy family. She'd clawed her way out of the slum and into the upper echelons of society—even if she'd only been a fringe member—and she'd studied and emulated everyone in this world until she'd had no trouble passing herself off as a pure-blooded member.

Tonight was no exception. She'd paid a not-so-small fortune to rent the crimson velvet Carolina Herrera gown and Dolce & Gabbana shoes, not to mention the Bulgari earrings and pendant and the black silk Valentino opera coat necessitated by the frigid December temperatures. The red hues, she knew, complemented her gray eyes and the dark blond hair that was long enough now to have been swept up into a French twist, held in place by a single hidden comb.

She lifted a hand to make sure every hair was in place, smiling at how much she enjoyed having it long. She'd worn it boyishly short all her life, until earlier this year, and hadn't sported her natural color since high school, when she'd dyed her hair black during her grunge phase and liked it enough to keep it that way. She hadn't even realized how it had deepened to such a beautiful honey-infused blond over the years.

Between her natural color and the new length—not to mention her rented duds—no one from the old neighborhood would recognize her tonight.

But she wasn't thinking about any of that, either, she reminded herself. Tonight really was going to be perfect. It really was going to be everything she had planned all those years ago.

Except maybe for the handsome, elegantly attired man the hostess had seated at a table near hers a few moments ago, and whom she hadn't been able to resist sneaking peeks at during each of those moments. When Della was a kid, she'd never entertained the idea of having a companion for her special evening. She wasn't sure why not. Maybe because of the aforementioned knowing she would always have only herself to count on. Or maybe because, as a kid, she couldn't even imagine a guy like him. In her neighborhood, *elegantly attired* had meant one's shirt was buttoned. And *handsome* had meant a guy had all his teeth.

Without warning, the man glanced up, his gaze connecting with hers. Something between the two of them…clicked. Or something. The man dipped his dark head toward Della in silent acknowledgment, one corner of his mouth lifting in something vaguely resembling a smile. After only a moment's hesitation, she lifted her glass in a silent toast to him. Swathed in a tuxedo that had been tailored to emphasize every magnificent inch of him, he was framed by billows of amber silk that edged the window behind him. His dark eyes were warmed by the dreamy light of the candle flickering in a crystal holder in front of him, and his little half smile sent a shudder of something hot and electric skittering down Della's spine. Because it was the kind of smile that told a woman he was not just undressing her with his eyes, but he was also considering using a lot of his other body parts on her, too.

When she felt the heat of a blush creep into her cheeks, she hastily glanced away. Lifting her champagne to her mouth for a cooling sip, she did her best to focus on something else—the crisp white tablecloths, the sparkling china, the glittering crowd. Inescapably, however, her attention wandered back to the man at the table opposite hers.

Who was still gazing at her with much interest.

"So what do you think?" he asked her, raising his voice enough to be heard two small tables away from his own.

Della blinked at him, nonplussed. Understanding, for the first time in her life, what *nonplussed* actually meant: confusion mixed with a funny little buzz in the belly that wasn't altogether unpleasant. A million different possible replies to his question ricocheted around in her brain. *I think you're the most beautiful man I've ever seen,* for example. And, *what are you doing New Year's Eve?* Even a smooth, *hey, lover.* And of course—it went without saying—*oh,* bay-*bee!*

"For dinner," he added, holding up the menu. "What do you recommend?"

Ooooh, what did Della think about *that?* Well, that was a totally different question from the one she'd been thinking he asked, wasn't it? Good thing she'd been too nonplussed to answer.

"Um, I'm not sure," she said. "This is the first time I've dined here." Somehow, she didn't think a man like him would be too impressed if she told him to order whatever was most expensive, because it would make him appear chic, sophisticated and rich. He was all those things simply by existing on the planet.

Her answer seemed to surprise him. "But how can this be your first time? Palumbo's has been a Chicago institution for nearly a hundred years. Are you not from Chicago originally?"

There was no way Della was going to answer that question. Mostly because no one other than Geoffrey knew she was here, and he was keeping much too close an eye on her. Even if he didn't know exactly where she was at the moment, she wasn't about to risk his discovery of her little escape by breathing a word of it to anyone.

So she wouldn't—couldn't—tell this man that. Either she'd have to lie—which Della never did, even though her honesty had gotten her into trouble more than once, as evidenced by her having to rely on Geoffrey at the moment—or else her reply would lead to the kind of small talk that might make her talk about her past. Or, even worse, her present. And she wanted to be as far removed from both of those tonight as she could be, on account of nothing in her past or present lent itself to Carolina Herrera gowns or diamonds and rubies or box seats to *La Bohème.*

So she replied instead to the first question he'd asked. "I ordered the special. I adore seafood."

He said nothing for a moment, and Della wondered if it was because he was pondering her answer to his first question or trying to decide whether or not to press the fact that she hadn't replied to the second. Finally, he said, "I'll remember that."

For some reason, though, he made it sound as if it were the fact that she loved seafood that he would remember, and not that she had recommended it for dinner.

He opened his mouth to say something else, but his server arrived to place a short, amber-colored cocktail in front of him and a dewy pink cosmopolitan on the table at the place directly next to his.

He was expecting someone to join him, Della realized. A woman, judging by the color and daintiness of the drink. Couples didn't dine in places like Palumbo's unless their relationship went beyond casual—or one of them was looking to make it more than casual. This guy was throwing steamy glances her way, even flirting with her, despite the fact that there would be a woman joining him momentarily. That meant the guy was a complete jerk.

Okay, so maybe her thirtieth birthday celebration wasn't going to go *quite* as perfectly as she had planned, since she was going to have to be seated near a jerk. And—*oh, all right*—maybe it wasn't only because of the jerk that the celebration wouldn't be exactly what she'd had in mind. Maybe it wasn't even because her gown and accessories were rentals from a Michigan Avenue boutique instead of pulled casually from her own closet.

Maybe, just maybe, it was because, in addition to not being the life of a millionaire, Della's current life wasn't even her own. Everything about her life these days—every thing she did, every place she went, every word she spoke—had to be vetted and controlled by Geoffrey. Her life would never be normal again. Or, at least, it would never be the life she had made for herself or the one she had planned. It would be a life manufactured and orchestrated by someone else.

As soon as the thought formed, she pushed it to the furthest, darkest recesses of her brain. She wouldn't think about any of that tonight, she reminded herself again, wondering why she was finding it all so hard to forget. Because tonight, she didn't want to be Della anyway. Tonight, for one night, she wanted to be the woman she had envisioned herself to be two decades and two thousand miles ago: CinderDella, toast of the town and belle of the ball. Nothing was going to mar this evening. Not even Prince Less-Than-Charming over there who was still making bedroom eyes at her while waiting on a girlfriend who could do a helluva lot better.

As if cued by the thought, the hostess seated a boisterous party of four at the table between them, completely blocking the man from her view. For that Della was grateful and not disappointed, even if some twisted part of her made her think that was what she was feeling.

Well, even if he was a jerk, he was still the most beautiful man she'd ever seen.

And she saw him again an hour and a half later—at the Lyric Opera when she was trying to locate her seat. After realizing she was in the wrong part of the auditorium, Della asked an usher for directions, then found herself gazing at a box across the room that afforded an amazing view of the stage…and where sat the handsome stranger she'd seen at dinner. Just as he'd been at the restaurant, he was surrounded by gold, this time a cascade of engraved gilt that encrusted the walls and ensconced the stage. Likewise as he'd been at the restaurant, he was seated alone.

Okay, so maybe as she'd left Palumbo's, Della had happened to notice that his date still hadn't shown up. Not that she'd been *trying* to notice that. She just had, that was all. Though whether the woman had gotten waylaid somewhere and been unable to make their rendezvous, or she'd wised up about what kind of man he was, Della couldn't have said.

Not that she cared either way. Hey, she'd barely noticed. In case she hadn't mentioned that.

Now as she strode down the aisle to her seat, she similarly barely noticed that it was not only in the same box the man was occupying, but also in the same row, as well—a small one at the front that contained only three chairs. She also barely noticed that he had placed both a program and a long-stemmed rose on the seat beside his own, as if the chair would soon be occupied. So evidently his girlfriend had indeed been waylaid earlier and was intending to catch up to him here.

Butterflies head-butted Della's midsection at the prospect of having to sit in such close proximity to the man. Once she squeezed past him to get to her seat, there would be no escaping him—unless she wanted to pull a Groucho Marx maneuver from *A Night at the Opera* and swing across the auditorium on a cable.

She inhaled a single, fortifying breath and forced her feet to move forward until she stood at the edge of the row beside him. His head snapped up, and, when he recognized her, he grinned that shudders-down-the-spine grin again. Heat flared in her belly, her brain turned to mush, and the *excuse me* Della had been about to utter evaporated in her mouth.

He murmured a greeting as he stood, but she barely heard it, because she was too busy trying not to swoon. Not only did he smell delectable—a luscious mix of spice and wood smoke—but he was also much taller than she'd realized, forcing her to tip back her head to meet his gaze. It was an action to which she was unaccustomed, since she pushed the six-foot mark herself in the two-inch heels she was wearing. Even without heels, she was accustomed to being at eye level with virtually everyone. With this man, however, eye level meant gazing at shoulders that spanned a distance roughly the size of Montana.

But it was his face that drew her attention. His jawline was resolute, his nose was straight and refined, his cheekbones looked as if they'd been hewn from marble, and his eyes… Oh, his eyes. His eyes were the color of bittersweet chocolate, a brown so dark and so compelling that Della couldn't tear her gaze away. Then she realized it wasn't the depth or color of his eyes that so captivated her. It was her recognition of something in them that was at odds with his dazzling smile. A somberness, even sadness, that was unmistakable.

The moment she identified it, however, a shadow fell over his eyes, almost as if he was aware of her understanding and didn't want her to see too deeply into him.

"We've got to stop meeting like this," he said, his smile broadening.

The humor in his tone surprised her, coming as it did on the heels of the shadows in his eyes. Even so, she couldn't quite keep herself from smiling back. "It is a little odd, isn't it?"

"Actually, I'm thinking of a different word."

Not sure that she wanted to know what it was, she heard herself ask anyway, "Oh?"

"Lucky," he said immediately. "I was thinking it was *lucky.*"

She wasn't sure what to say in response to that, so she held up her ticket and gestured toward her seat. She made sure to give the rose-laden chair between hers and his a meaningful inspection before saying, "If you don't mind? That's my seat."

For a minute, he only continued to gaze at her,

his eyes revealing nothing now of what might be going through his head. Then, "Not at all," he replied, sidestepping into the aisle to give her room to pass.

When he did, she hastened to take her seat, immediately opening her program to read it before he had a chance to say anything that might start a conversation.

He didn't take the hint, however, and said as he returned to his seat, "How was your dinner?"

Not looking up from the program, Della replied, "Lovely."

Her one-word response did nothing to dissuade him, either. "I ended up ordering the pheasant. It was amazing."

When Della only nodded silently without looking up from her program, he added, "You should try it next time you're at Palumbo's. I highly recommend it."

He was fishing. Trying to find out if she lived here in town the same way he had when he'd asked her why she'd never been to Palumbo's. He was trying to gauge whether or not there was a chance the two of them might run into each other again, either by accident or by design. Even with a long-stemmed rose and mystery woman between them.

"I'll take it under advisement," she told him. And returned to reading her program.

But still, he didn't take the hint. "You know, I don't meet many people of my own generation who enjoy opera," he said, trying a new tack. "Especially not enough to see it performed live. Or spring for box seats. You must really love it."

Della sighed inwardly, silently cursing him for the change of subject. That was a low blow. There was no way she could resist a conversation about her most favorite thing in the world.

"I adore it, actually," she said helplessly, letting the program fall open onto her lap.

When she turned to look at him again, his expression made clear he was as delighted to be here as she was and that he felt every bit as passionately about opera. So passionately that his love for the medium had chased away the darkness that had clouded his eyes earlier. She realized now that they weren't entirely brown. Flecks of gold wreathed the irises, making his eyes appear more faceted somehow, drawing her in even more deeply.

"I've loved opera since I was a little girl," she told him. "Our next-door neighbor was a huge fan and introduced me to all the classics." She didn't add that that was only because she could hear Mrs. Klosterman's radio through the paper-thin walls of their tenement, or how Della had hung on every word of the announcer's analysis of each opera once it had concluded. "The first time I saw one performed live," she continued, not bothering to mention that it was live on PBS, not live on stage, "I was enchanted."

She actually would have loved to major in music and make the study of opera her life's work. But college had been beyond the means of an average student from her economic stratum, so she'd gone directly to work after graduating from high school, as a gofer in the offices of one of Wall Street's most noted and respected brokerage houses. And even though she'd worked her way up the corporate ladder to become an executive assistant, Della had never made the time to go for the degree. She'd been supporting herself fairly well on her salary—certainly better than she'd ever imagined she would growing up in the sort of neighborhood she had—and she'd been happy with the way her life was going. At least until that life had shattered into a million pieces, and she'd been left with nothing but Geoffrey, who'd offered her a dubious sort of refuge—and not without a price.

Almost as if that thought had cued the orchestra, the music swelled, and the lights dimmed. Della couldn't resist one last look at her companion as the room grew dark, but when she saw him gazing at her—and noted the seat between them still empty—she quickly turned her attention to the stage.

After that, she fell into the world of Mimi and Rodolfo and their bohemian friends, leaving her own reality behind. So much so, that when the lights came up for intermission, it took Della a moment to return from nineteenth century Paris to twenty-first century Chicago. She blinked a few times and inhaled a deep breath and, before she could stop herself, looked over at her companion—who was looking at her in the same way he had been when the lights had dimmed, almost as if he'd spent the entire first half of the opera watching her instead.

That strange buzz erupted in her belly again, so she quickly glanced at the crowd. The myriad splendor of the women's gowns made them look like brightly colored gems amid the gilt of the auditorium, the sparkle of their jewelry only enhancing the image. Della watched many of the ladies link arms with their companions as they left for intermission, and noted how the men bent their heads affectionately toward them as they laughed or chatted.

For a moment, she felt a keen regret that this night couldn't last forever. Wouldn't it be lovely to enjoy evenings like this whenever she wanted, without regard for their cost or the risk of being seen in a place where she shouldn't be? She couldn't remember the last time she'd had a night out at all, never mind one like this. Geoffrey kept her locked away like Rapunzel. She spent her time reading books, watching downloaded movies and staring at the walls that were, for all intents and purposes, her cell. Even if the place Geoffrey had provided lacked bars and held sufficient creature comforts, Della still felt like a prisoner. Hell, she was a prisoner. And she would be until Geoffrey told her she could go.

But even that thought brought little comfort, because she had no idea *where* she would go, or what she would do, once Geoffrey decided she was no longer necessary. She would have to start all over again with virtually nothing. The same way she had when she left the old neighborhood behind.

It was all the more reason to enjoy tonight to the fullest, Della told herself. Who knew what the future held beyond even the next few hours?

"So what do you think so far?"

She turned at the sound of the rich, velvety baritone, and her pulse rippled when she saw the smoky look he was giving her. Truly, she had to get a grip. Not only did the guy show evidence of being a class-A heel, flirting with one woman when he was supposed to be out with another, but he was also way out of Della's league.

"I have to confess that *La Bohème* isn't one of my favorites," she admitted. "I think Puccini was a bit reserved when he scored it, especially when you compare it to the exhilaration of something like *Manon Lescaut*. But I am enjoying it. Very much."

Of course, some of that might have had to do with the company seated in her box. Not that she had to tell him that. Not that she had to admit it to herself.

"How about you?" she asked. "What's your verdict?"

"I think I've seen it too many times to be objective anymore," he said. "But it's interesting you say that about Puccini's being too reserved with it. I've always kind of thought the same thing. I actually like Leoncavallo's interpretation of Murger's book much better."

She grinned. "I do, too."

He grinned back. "That puts us in the minority, you know."

"I know."

"In fact," he added, "I like Leoncavallo's *La Bohème* even better than his *Pagliacci,* an opinion that will get you tossed out of some opera houses."

She laughed at that. "I like it better than *Pagliacci,* too. Looks like we'll be kicked to the curb together."

He chuckled lightly, both of them quieting at the same time, neither seeming to know what to say next. After a couple of awkward seconds, Della ventured, "Well, if you've already seen *La Bohème* too many times, and you don't care for it as much as you do other operas, then why are you here tonight?"

He shrugged, but there was something in the gesture that was in no way careless, and the warmth that had eased his expression fled. "I have season tickets."

Tickets, she repeated to herself. Not *ticket.* Plural, not singular. Meaning he was indeed the owner of the empty seat beside his and had been expecting someone to occupy it tonight. Someone who might very well be with him all the other nights of the season. A wife, perhaps?

She hastily glanced at his left hand but saw no ring. Still, there were plenty of married people who eschewed the ring thing these days. Della wondered who normally joined him and why she wasn't here tonight. She waited to see if he would add something about the mysteriously empty chair. Something that might clarify the sudden drop in temperature that seemed to shimmer between them. Because she sensed that that vacant chair was what had generated the faint chill.

Instead, he shook off his odd, momentary funk and said, "That is how I know you don't normally attend Lyric Opera performances. At least not on opening night, and not in the seat you're sitting in tonight." He smiled again, and the chill abated some. "I would have noticed."

She did her best to ignore the butterflies doing the rumba in her stomach. "This is my first time coming here," she confessed.

His inspection of her grew ponderous. "Your first time at Palumbo's. Your first time at the Lyric. So you have just moved to Chicago recently, haven't you?"

She was saved from having to reply, because the opera gods and goddesses—Wagnerian, she'd bet, every one of them—smiled down on her. Her companion was beckoned from below by a couple who had recognized him and wanted to say hello—and who addressed him as Marcus, giving Della his first name, at least. Then they proceeded to say way more than hello to him, chatting until the lights flickered once, twice, three times, indicating that the performance was about to resume. At that, the couple scurried off, and he—Marcus—turned to look at Della again.

"Can you see all right from where you are?" he asked. He patted the chair next to him that still contained the unopened program and rose. "You might have a better vantage point from this seat. You want to have the best angle for 'Addio Dolce Svegliare Alla Mattina.'"

The Italian rolled off his tongue as if he spoke it fluently, and a ribbon of something warm and gooey unfurled in her. Even though the vantage point would be no different from the one she had now—which he must realize, too—Della was surprised by how much she wanted to accept his offer. Whoever usually sat there obviously wasn't coming. And he didn't seem to be as bothered by that as a man involved in a romantic relationship should be. So maybe his relationship with the usual occupant of the chair wasn't romantic, in spite of the red, red rose.

Or maybe he was just a big ol' hound dog with whom she'd be better off not sharing anything more than opera chitchat. Maybe he should only be another lovely, momentary memory to go along with all the other lovely, momentary memories she was storing from this evening.

"Thank you, but the view from here is fine," she said.

And it was, she told herself. For now. For tonight.

But not, unfortunately, forever.

Two

Marcus Fallon sat in his usual seat at his usual table drinking his usual nightcap in his usual club, thinking the most unusual thoughts. Or, at least, thoughts about a most unusual woman. A woman unlike any he'd ever met before. And not only because she shared his passion for, and opinions about, opera, either. Unfortunately, the moment the curtain had fallen on *La Bohème,* she'd hurried past him with a breathlessly uttered *good night,* scurried up the aisle ahead of everyone else in the box and he'd lost her in the crowd before he'd been able to say a word. He'd experienced a moment of whimsy as he'd scanned the stairs on his way out looking for a glass slipper, but even that small fairy-tale clue had eluded him. She was gone. Just like that. Almost as if she'd never been there at all. And he had no idea how to find her.

He lifted his Scotch to his lips again, filling his mouth with the smooth, smoky liquor, scanning the crowd here as if he were looking for her again. Strangely, he realized he was. But all he saw was the usual crowd milling around the dark-paneled, richly appointed, sumptuously decorated room. Bernie Stegman was, as usual, sitting in an oxblood leather wingback near the fireplace, chatting up Lucas Whidmore, who sat in an identical chair on the other side. Delores and Marion Hagemann were having a late dinner with Edith and Lawrence Byck at their usual table in the corner, the quartet framed by heavy velvet drapes the color of old money. Cynthia Harrison was doing her usual flirting with Stu, the usual Saturday bartender, who was sidestepping her advances with his usual aplomb. He would lose his job if he were caught canoodling with the patrons.

Thoughts of canoodling brought Marcus's ruminations back to the mysterious lady in red. Not that that was entirely surprising, since the minute he'd seen her sitting opposite him at Palumbo's, canoodling had been at the forefront of his brain. She'd simply been that stunning. What was really strange, though, was that once he'd started talking to her at the Lyric, canoodling had fallen by the wayside, and what he'd really wanted to do with her was talk more about opera. And not only because she shared his unconventional opinions, either. But because of the way she'd lit up while talking about it. As beautiful as she'd been, seated alone at her table in the restaurant, she'd become radiant during their conversation.

Radiant, he repeated to himself, frowning. Now there was a word he'd never used to describe a woman before. Then again, that could be because he'd seldom moved past the stage with a woman where he found her beautiful. Meaning he'd seldom reached a stage where he actually talked to one. Once he bedded a woman—and that usually came pretty early after meeting one—he lost interest. But that was because few women were worth knowing beyond the biblical sense.

Unbidden, a reproving voice erupted in his brain, taking him to task for his less-than-stellar commentary, but it wasn't his own. It was Charlotte's sandpaper rasp, made that way by too many cigarettes over the course of her eighty-two years. More than once over the past two decades since making her acquaintance, he'd let slip some politically incorrect comment about the opposite sex, only to have her haul him up by his metaphorical collar—and sometimes by his not-so-metaphorical collar—to set him straight.

God, he missed her.

He glanced at the pink cosmopolitan sitting opposite his single malt on the table, the glass dewy with condensation since it had been sitting there for so long. The rose, too, had begun to wilt, its petals blackening at their edges. Even the opera program looked limp and tattered already. All of them were at the end of their lives. Just as Charlotte had been the last time he'd sat at this table looking in the same direction.

She'd died two days after closing night at the Lyric. It had been seven months since her funeral, and Marcus still felt her loss keenly. He wondered, not for the first time, what happened after a soul left this world to enter the next. Was Charlotte still able to enjoy her occasional cosmo? Did they have performances of Verdi and Bizet where she was now? And was she able to enjoy the rare prime rib she'd loved to order at Palumbo's?

Marcus hoped so. Charlotte deserved only the best, wherever she was. Because the best was what she had always given him.

A flash of red caught his eye, and Marcus glanced up. But it was only Emma Stegman, heading from the bar toward her father. Marcus scanned the room again for good measure but saw only more of the usual suspects. He knew everyone here, he thought. So why was he sitting alone? Hell, Stu the bartender wasn't the only guy Cynthia Harrison had tried canoodling with. If Marcus wanted to, he could sidle up next to her and be headed to the Ambassador Hotel, which was adjacent to the club, in no time. And he sure wouldn't lose his job for it. All he'd lose would be the empty feeling inside that had been with him since Charlotte's death. Of course, the feeling would come back tomorrow, when he was alone again….

He lifted his glass and downed what was left of his Scotch, then, for good measure, downed Charlotte's cosmopolitan, too, in one long gulp. He squeezed his eyes shut for a moment as he waited for the taste to leave his mouth—how had she stood those things?—then opened them again…

…to see a vision in red seated at a table on the other side of the room. He could not believe his good fortune. Seeing her one time had been chance. Seeing her twice had been lucky. Seeing her a third time…

That could only be fate.

Forgetting, for now, that he didn't believe in such a thing, and before he risked losing her again, he immediately rose and crossed to where she was seated, signaling for Stu at the same time and gesturing toward her table. Without waiting to be invited, he pulled out the chair across from hers and seated himself.

She glanced up at his appearance, surprise etched on her features. But her lips curled into the faintest of smiles, reassuring him. That was another new experience for him. He'd never had to be reassured of anything. On the contrary, he'd taken everything in life for granted. That was what happened when you were born into one of the Gold Coast's oldest and most illustrious families. You got everything you wanted, often without even having to ask for it. In fact, you even got the things you didn't ask for. Usually handed to you on a silver platter. Sometimes literally.

"We have got to stop meeting like this."

This time it was she, not Marcus, who spoke the words he had said to her at the Lyric.

"On the contrary," he replied. "I'm beginning to like meeting you like this."

A hint of pink bloomed on her cheeks at his remark, and delight wound through his belly at seeing her blush. He couldn't remember the last time he'd made a woman blush. Not shyly, anyway. Not becomingly. Usually, if he made a woman blush, it was because he'd suggested they do something in the bedroom that most of society considered shameful. It was all the more reason, in his opinion, why it should be enjoyed.

But he was getting way ahead of himself. Anything in the bedroom with this woman was still, oh…hours away.

"Mind if I join you?" he asked.

"I think you already have."

He feigned surprise. "So I have. Then you'll have to let me buy you a drink."

She opened her mouth to reply and, for a moment, he feared she would decline his offer. Another new experience for Marcus. Not only fearing a woman would turn him down—since that almost never happened—but also feeling a knot of disappointment in his chest at the possibility. On those rare occasions when a woman did turn him down, he simply shrugged it off and moved to the next one. Because, inevitably, there was always a next one. With this woman, however…

Well, he couldn't imagine a next one. Not even

with Cynthia Harrison falling out of her dress less than ten feet away.

"All right," she finally said, as Stu arrived at their table. She looked at the bartender. "I'll have a glass of champagne, please."

"Bring a bottle," Marcus instructed before the bartender had a chance to get away. "The Perrier-Jouët Cuvée Belle Epoque. 2002."

"Really, that's not necessary…." she began, her voice trailing off on the last word.

Deciding it was because she didn't know how to address him—and because he wanted to give her his name so that he could get hers in return— he finished for her, "Marcus. Marcus—"

"Don't tell me your last name."

He halted before revealing it, less because she asked him not to than because he found her command curious.

"Why not?"

"Just don't, that's all."

He started to give it to her anyway—never let it be said that Marcus Fallon ever did as he was told—but for some reason decided to honor her request. That was even stranger, since never let it be said that Marcus Fallon did the honorable thing, either. "All right." He lifted his right hand for her to shake. "And you are…?"

She hesitated before taking his hand, then gingerly placed her own lightly against his. Her fingers were slender and delicate against his large, blunt ones and, unable to help himself, he closed his hand possessively over hers. Her skin was soft and warm, as creamy as ivory, and he found himself wondering if that was true of the rest of her. The blush on her cheeks deepened as he covered her hand with his, but she didn't pull hers away.

His appeal for her name hung in the air between them without a response. "Della," she told him finally. "My name is Della."

No last name from her, either, then. Fine, he thought. He wouldn't push it. But before the night was over, he'd know not only her last name, but everything else about her, too. Especially where each and every one of her erogenous zones were and what kind of erotic sounds she uttered whenever he located a new one.

Neither of them said anything more, only studied each other's faces as their hands remained joined. She had amazing eyes. Pale, clear gray, the kind of eyes a man could lose himself in forever. The kind that hid nothing and said much. Honest eyes, he finally decided. Noble. The eyes of a person who would always do the right thing.

Damn.

Stu cleared his throat a little too obviously beside them, and she gave a soft tug to free her fingers. Reluctantly, he let them go. She lowered her hand to the table near his, however, resting it palm down on the white linen. So he did likewise, flattening his hand until his fingers almost—almost—touched hers.

"Will there be anything else, Mr.—?" Stu stopped before revealing Marcus's last name, obviously having overheard the exchange. Quickly, he amended, "Will there be anything else, sir?"

Marcus waved a hand airily in his direction, muttering that Stu should bring some kind of appetizer, too, but didn't specify what. He honestly didn't care about anything, other than the intriguing woman who sat across from him.

"Well," he began, trying to jump-start the

conversation again. "If you're sitting here in the Windsor Club, you can't be too new to Chicago. They have a waiting list to get in, and last I heard, it was two years, at least, before anyone added to it could even expect an application. Unless you're here as a guest of another member?" That would be just his luck. That he'd meet a woman like this, and she'd be involved with someone else.

"I'm on my own," she told him. Then, after a small hesitation, she added, "Tonight."

Suggesting she wasn't on her own on other nights, Marcus thought. For the first time, it occurred to him to glance down at her left hand. Not that a wedding ring had ever stopped him from seducing a woman before. But she sported only one ring, and it was on her right hand. The left bore no sign of ever having had one. So she wasn't even engaged. At least not to a man who had the decency to buy her a ring.

"Or maybe," he continued thoughtfully, "you're a member of one of the Windsor's original charter families who earn and keep their membership by a simple accident of birth." He grinned. "Like me. As many times as they've tried to throw me out of this place, they can't."

She grinned back. "And why on earth would they throw out a paragon of formality and decency like you?"

His eyebrows shot up at that. "You really are new in town if no one's warned you about me yet. That's usually the first thing they tell beautiful young socialites. In fact, ninety percent of the tourist brochures for the city say something like, 'Welcome to Chicago. While you're here, be sure to visit Navy Pier, the Hancock Tower, the Field Museum and the Shedd Aquarium. And whatever you do, stay away from Marcus—" Again he halted before saying his last name. "Well, stay away from Marcus-Whose-Last-Name-You-Don't-Want-To-Know. That guy's nothing but trouble.'"

She laughed at that. She had a really great laugh. Uninhibited, unrestrained, genuinely happy. "And what do the other ten percent of the travel brochures say?"

"Well, those would be the ones they give out to conventioneers looking for a good time while they're away from the ball and chain. Those are the ones that list all the, ah, less seemly places in town." He smiled again. "I'm actually featured very prominently in those. Not by name, mind you, but…" He shrugged. "Those damned photographers don't care who they take pictures of."

She laughed again, stirring something warm and fizzy inside Marcus unlike anything he'd ever felt before. "I don't believe you," she said. "I find it hard to jibe *The Bartered Bride* with bump and grind."

"There's more to me than opera, you know." He met her gaze levelly. "A lot more."

The blush blossomed in her cheeks again, making him chuckle more softly. She was saved from having to respond to his comment, however, when Stu arrived with their champagne and a tray of fruit and cheese. The bartender went a little overboard with the presentation and opening of the bottle, but it was probably because he, too, recognized that Della—yes, Marcus did like that name—wasn't a usual customer. In fact, there was nothing usual about her. She was, in a word, extraordinary.

After receiving approval for the champagne, Stu poured a glass for each of them. As he did, Marcus told Della, "I am notorious in this town. Ask anyone."

She turned to the bartender, who was nestling the champagne in a silver bucket of ice. "Is he really notorious?" she asked.

The bartender glanced first at Marcus, who nodded imperceptibly to let Stu know his tip wouldn't be compromised by his honesty, then at Della. "Oh, yes, ma'am. And not just in Chicago. He makes the society pages all over the country, wherever he goes, and he's a regular feature on a lot of those celebrity websites. If you're seen with him, it's a good bet you'll wind up there yourself. He's infamous."

Della turned to Marcus, her eyes no longer full of laughter, but now brimming with something akin to…fear? Oh, surely not. What would she have to be afraid of?

"Is that true?" she asked.

Still puzzled by her reaction, but not wanting to lie to her—especially since it would be easy enough for her to find out with a simple internet search—he told her, "I'm afraid so."

Her lips parted fractionally, and her expression became almost panicked. Deciding she must be feigning fear as a joke, he played along, telling her, "Don't worry. They never let riffraff like the paparazzi into the club. You're perfectly safe with me here. No one will see you with me."

It occurred to him as he said it that that was exactly what she feared—being seen with him. Not just by the paparazzi, but by some individual in particular. An individual who might not like seeing her out with Marcus. Or anyone else, for that matter.

She did have that look about her, he decided as he considered her again. Pampered, well tended to, cared for—at least on the surface. The kind of woman who made her way in the world by making herself available to men who could afford her. There were still a surprising number of such women in society, even in this day and age when a woman shouldn't have to rely on her sexuality to make her way in the world. Beautiful, elegant, reserved, they tended to be. At least on the surface.

Not that he'd ever seen Della among such women in the level of society in which he traveled. That only fueled his suspicion that she was merely visiting the city. Dammit.

It took a moment for her expression to clear, but she finally emitted a single—albeit a tad humorless—chuckle. "Of course," she said. "I mean…I knew that. I was only kidding."

He nodded, but there was a part of him that wasn't quite convinced. Maybe she really was attached to someone else. Maybe she even *belonged* to that someone. Maybe that someone wouldn't be too happy about her being here tonight alone. Or anywhere alone. Maybe that someone would be even more unhappy to find her with another man. Maybe she really was afraid her photo would show up somewhere with Marcus at her side, and she'd be in big, big trouble with that someone.

Just who was she, this mysterious lady in red? And why did Marcus want so badly to find out?

In an effort to dispel the odd tension that had

erupted between them, he lifted his glass of champagne and said, softly, "Cheers."

There was another small hesitation on her part before, she, too, lifted her glass. "Cheers," she echoed even more softly.

The toast didn't put an end to the frisson of uneasiness that still hovered over the table, but it did put a bit of the bloom back in her cheeks. It was enough, he decided. For now.

But certainly not forever.

Della gazed at the man seated across the table from her as she sipped her champagne, and she wondered exactly when the evening had jumped the track and started screeching headlong into a dark, scary tunnel. One minute, she'd been about to embark on the last leg of her evening by enjoying a final glass of champagne at Chicago's celebrated Windsor Club—which she'd gotten into only by bribing the doorman with another small fortune—and the next minute, she'd found herself gazing once again into the gold-flecked, chocolate-brown eyes that had so intrigued her at the opera.

Marcus. His name fit him. Stoic and classic, commanding and uncompromising. How strange that she should run into him at every destination she'd visited tonight. Then again, she'd gone out of her way to choose destinations that were magnets for the rich and powerful, and he certainly fit that bill. Of course, now she was learning he was part of that other adjective that went along with rich—*famous*—and that was a condition she most definitely had to avoid.

So what was she afraid of? He was right. There was no one in the club who didn't belong here. Other than herself, she meant. Nobody had even seemed to notice the two of them. Not to mention it was late and, even if it was Saturday, ninety percent of the city's population had gone home. There was snow in the forecast for later, even if it wasn't anything a city like Chicago couldn't handle. Most people were probably hunkered down in their living rooms and bedrooms, having stocked up on provisions earlier, and were looking forward to a Sunday being snowed in with nothing to do.

Della wished she could enjoy something like

that, but she felt as though she'd been snowed in with nothing to do for the past eleven months. At least when she wasn't at Geoffrey's beck and call.

But tonight that wasn't the case. Tonight she was having fun. She should look at the opportunity to share the last couple of hours of her celebration with a man like Marcus as the icing on her birthday cake.

"So…" she began, trying to recapture the flirtatiousness of their earlier exchange. Still trying to figure out when, exactly, she'd decided to return his flirtations. "What kinds of things have you done to make yourself so notorious?"

He savored another sip of his champagne, then placed the glass on the table between them. But instead of releasing it, he dragged his fingers up over the stem and along the bowl of the flute, then up farther along the elegant line of its sides. Della found herself mesmerized by the voyage of those fingers, especially when he began to idly trace the rim with the pad of his middle finger. Around and around it went, slowly, slowly…oh, so slowly…until a coil of heat began to unwrap in her belly and purl into parts beyond.

She found herself wondering what it would be like to have him drawing idle circles like that elsewhere, someplace like, oh…she didn't know. Herself maybe. Along her shoulder, perhaps. Or down her thigh. Touching her in other places, too—places where such caresses might drive her to the brink of madness.

Her eyes fluttered closed as the thought formed in her brain, as if by not watching what he was doing, she might better dispel the visions dancing around in her head. But closing her eyes only made those images more vivid. More earthy. More erotic. More…*oh.* So much more *more.* She snapped her eyes open again in an effort to squash the visions completely. But that left her looking at Marcus, who was gazing at her with faint amusement, as if he'd seen where her attention had settled and knew exactly what she was thinking about.

As he studied her, he stilled his finger on the rim of the glass and settled his index finger beside it. Della watched helplessly as he scissored them along the rim, first opening, then closing, then opening again. With great deliberation, he curled them into the glass until they touched the top of the champagne, then he dampened each finger with the effervescent wine. Then he carefully pulled them out and lifted them to her lips, brushing lightly over her mouth with the dew of champagne.

Heat swamped her, making her stomach simmer, her breasts tingle and her heart rate quadruple, and dampening her between her legs. Without even thinking about what she was doing, she parted her lips enough to allow him to tuck one finger inside. She tasted the champagne then, along with the faint essence of Marcus. And Marcus was, by far, the most intoxicating.

Quickly, she drew her head back and licked the remnants of his touch from her lips. Not that that did anything to quell her arousal. What had come over her? How could she be this attracted to a man this quickly? She knew almost nothing about him, save his name and the fact that he loved opera and good champagne and had bought a rose for someone earlier in the evening who—

The rose. How could she have forgotten about that? She might very well be sitting here enjoying the advances of a married man! Or, at the very least, one who belonged to someone else. And the last thing she wanted to be was part of a triangle.

Where was the rose now? Had he thrown it resentfully into the trash or pressed it between the pages of the neglected opera program as a keepsake? Involuntarily, she scanned the other tables in the club until she saw an empty one not far away with a rose and opera program lying atop it. And another martini glass—though this time it was empty. Had the woman he was expecting finally caught up with him? Had he only moments ago been sharing a moment like this with someone else? Could he really be that big a heel?

"Who were you expecting tonight?"

The question was out of her mouth before Della even realized it had formed in her brain.

It obviously surprised Marcus as much as it had her, because his dark eyebrows shot up again.

"No one," he told her. And then, almost as if he couldn't stop himself, he added, "Not even you. I could never have anticipated someone like you."

"But the rose… The pink drink…"

He turned to follow the track of her gaze, saw the table where he must have been sitting when she came in. His shoulders drooped a little, and his head dipped forward, as if in defeat. Or perhaps melancholy? When he looked at her, the shadows she'd noted before were back in his eyes. Definitely the latter.

"I did buy the rose and order the drink for someone else," he said. "And yes, she was someone special."

"Was?" Della echoed. "Then you and she aren't…"

"What?"

"Together?"

His expression revealed nothing of what he might be feeling or thinking. "No."

She wanted to ask more about the woman, but

something in his demeanor told her not to. It was none of her business, she reminded herself. It was bad enough she'd brought up memories for him that clearly weren't happy. Whoever the woman was, it was obvious she wasn't a part of his life anymore. Even if it was likewise obvious that he still wanted her to be.

And why did that realization prick her insides so much? Della wouldn't even see Marcus again after tonight. It didn't matter if he cared deeply for someone else, and the less she knew about him, the better. That way, he would be easier to forget.

Even if he was the kind of man a woman never forgot.

In spite of her relinquishing the subject, he added, "I knew she wouldn't be coming tonight, but it felt strange not to buy the rose and order her a drink the way I always did before. She always ran late," he added parenthetically and, Della couldn't help but note, affectionately. "It felt almost as if I were betraying her somehow not ordering for her, when really she was the one who—" He halted abruptly and met Della's gaze again. But now he didn't look quite so grim. "An uncharacteristic bout of sentimentality on my part, I guess. But no, Della. I'm not with anyone." He hesitated a telling moment before asking, "Are you?"

Well, now, there was a loaded question if ever there was one. Della wasn't with anyone—not the way Marcus meant it, anyway. She hadn't been with anyone that way for nearly a year. And that one had been someone she never should have been with in the first place. Not just because of the sort of man Egan Collingwood turned out to be, either. But Della was indeed with someone—in a different way. She was with Geoffrey. For now, anyway. And as long as she was with Geoffrey, there was no way she could be with anyone else.

She didn't want to tell Marcus that, though, so she only lifted her champagne to her lips for another sip. When he continued to study her in that inquisitive way, she enjoyed another sip. And another. And another. Until—would you look at that?—the glass was completely empty. The moment she set it on the table, however, Marcus poured her a refill, allowing the champagne to almost reach to the brim before lowering the bottle.

She grinned at the ridiculously full glass. "Marcus, are you trying to get me drunk?"

"Yes," he replied immediately.

His frankness surprised her, and she laughed. Honestly, she couldn't remember the last time she'd laughed so much in one evening. Even before Egan, she hadn't been so prone to jollity. She'd never even used a word like *jollity* before.

"Well, it won't work," she said, even as she carefully lifted the glass to her mouth. "I have a remarkable metabolism."

Now his smile turned faintly predatory. "I'm counting on that, actually."

Yikes.

Well, the joke was on him. Because Mr. Marcus Notorious might think he had the evening mapped out with the quickest route from chance dinner meeting to white-hot marathon of sex, but there was no way that was going to happen. Della had to have her rented clothes back tomorrow when Talk of the Town opened at noon or she'd lose her deposit. Even the promise of a white-hot marathon of sex with a maddeningly irresistible guy wasn't going to keep her from forgetting that.

She looked at Marcus, at his smoldering eyes and sizzling grin. At the brutally strong jaw and ruthless cheekbones. As if trying to counter the ruggedness of his features, an unruly lock of dark hair had tumbled carelessly over his forehead, begging for the gentling of a woman's fingers.

Well. Probably that wasn't going to keep her from getting her deposit. Hmm. Actually, that was kind of a tough call….

But then, Della couldn't spend the night doing anything anywhere, anyway. As it was, if Geoffrey called the house tonight and she didn't answer, he'd be hopping mad. Of course, he'd only have to call her on her cell phone to know she was okay, but he'd be furious that she wasn't cloistered where she was supposed to be. She'd been lucky enough so far that he hadn't ever called the house when she'd snuck out on those handful of occasions when she became bored to the point of lunacy. But she wasn't sure how much longer her luck would hold. If Geoffrey ever got wind of her excursions, he'd want to wring her neck. Then he'd become even more determined to keep her hidden.

Still looking at Marcus, but trying not to think about the way he was making her feel, she leaned back in her chair and said, "So you get women drunk and then take advantage of them. Now I know the kinds of things you've done to make yourself so notorious."

"Oh, I never have to get women drunk to take advantage, Della," he said with complete confidence and without an ounce of arrogance. "In fact, I never have to take advantage."

She had no doubt that was true. She'd just met the man, and she was already having thoughts about him and inclinations toward him she shouldn't be having. Too many thoughts. And *way* too many inclinations.

"Then what does make you so notorious?"

He leaned forward, bracing his elbows on the table as he invaded her space, effectively erasing what meager distance she'd put between them.

"Where do I begin?" he asked. "And, more important, do you have all night?"

Double yikes.

Having no idea what to say to that, she lifted her champagne for another idle sip…only to enjoy a healthy quaff instead. Well, it was very good. And she was starting to feel a lovely little buzz that was buffing the rough edges off…oh, everything.

As if he realized the turn her thoughts had taken, Marcus pushed his hand across the table until his fingertips were touching hers. A spark shot through Della, even at that simple, innocent touch. And when his hand crept up over hers, that spark leaped into a flame.

"Because if you *do* have all night," he added, "I'd be more than happy to give you a *very* thorough illustration."

Triple yikes. And another quaff, for good measure.

Ah, that was better. Now, what was it she had been about to say? Something about needing to get home because it was approaching midnight and, any minute now, she was going to turn into a bumpkin. Um, she meant pumpkin. Not that that was much better.

She searched for something to say that would extricate her from her predicament, but no words came. Probably because no ideas came. And probably no ideas came because they were all being crowded out by the visions featuring her and Marcus that kept jumping to the forefront of her brain. He really was incredibly sexy. And it had been such a long time since she'd been with anyone who turned her on the way he did. And it would probably be even longer before she found someone she wanted to be with again. She had no idea what would happen once Geoffrey was done with her. All she had that was certain was right now. This place. This moment. This man. This sexy, notorious, willing man. This man she should in no way allow herself to succumb to. This man who would haunt her for the rest of her life.

This man who, for some reason, she couldn't bring herself to leave quite yet….

Three

Della tore her gaze from his, forcing herself to look at something—anything—other than Marcus. Gazing past him, she found herself looking at the windows of two French doors not far from their table. The snow the forecasters had promised earlier in the day had begun to fall—delicate, dazzling flecks of white shimmering in the lamplight outside. As a native New Yorker, Della was no stranger to snow. And Chicago had seen snow more than once already this season. But there was something as magical to her about snow today as there had been when she was a child. When it had snowed then, at least for a little while, her neighborhood ceased to be a broken landscape of grimy concrete and asphalt and would transform into an enchanted world of sparkling white. The rusty fire escape outside her bedroom window morphed into a diamond-covered staircase that led to the top of an imprisoned princess's turret. The piles of garbage at the curb turned into pillows of glittering fairy-dust. The corroded cars became pearly silver coaches. Snow drove the gangs and dealers inside, who preyed on the neighborhood like wicked witches and evil sorcerers, so that all Della could see for block after block were radiant castles of white.

At least for a little while.

How appropriate that it should snow tonight, when she was actually enjoying the sort of enchanted adventure she'd had to invent as a child. How strangely right it felt to see those fat, fantastic flakes falling behind the man who had been such a bewitching Prince Charming this evening.

"It's snowing," she said softly.

Marcus turned to follow her gaze, then looked

at Della again. His expression indicated that snow didn't hold the same fascination or whimsical appeal for him that it did for her.

"They're predicting four or five inches," he said, sounding disappointed at the change of subject.

He looked down at their hands, at how his rested atop hers and how hers just lay there. With clear reluctance, he pulled his toward himself. It was what she wanted, Della told herself. A change in subject to change her feelings instead of changing her mind. So why did his withdrawal have the opposite effect? Why did she want him to take her hand again, only this time turn it so their palms were flat against each other and their fingers entwined?

Still, he didn't retreat completely. His fingertips still brushed hers, and she could feel the warmth of his skin clinging to her own. It was all she could do not to reach for him and arrange their hands the way they'd been before.

It was for the best, she told herself again. This was a momentary encounter. A momentary exchange. A momentary everything. Especially now that the snow had begun, she really should be leaving. She'd told the driver of her hired car that she would be at the club only until midnight. It was nearing that now. She definitely needed to wind down this…whatever it was…with Marcus. Then she needed to be on her way.

So why wasn't she?

"It will be just enough snow to turn everything into an ungodly mess," Marcus said distastefully, giving her the perfect segue she needed to say her farewells. Unfortunately, he added, "At least no one will have to battle rush hour to get to work," reminding her that tomorrow was Sunday, so it wasn't as though she had to get up *that* early. She could squeeze in another moment or two….

"By afternoon," he continued, "the city will be one big pile of black slush. Snow is nothing but a pain in the—"

"I love snow. I think it's beautiful."

Marcus smiled indulgently. "Spoken like someone who's never had to maneuver in it," he replied. Then he brightened. "But with that clue, I can add to my knowledge of you. I now know that, not only have you only arrived in Chicago recently, but you came here from some hot, sunny place that never has to worry about the hassle of snow."

She said nothing to contradict him. It wasn't lying when you didn't say anything. And the more misconceptions he had about her, the better.

At her silence, he grinned with much satisfaction. "I'm right, aren't I? You came here from someplace where it's hot all the time, didn't you?"

Oh, if he only knew. It had certainly been "hot" for her in New York when she left. Just not the way he meant. So she only smiled and said, "Guilty."

And not only of being from a "hot" place. She was guilty of twisting the truth in an effort to stay honest with him. Guilty of letting him believe she was someone she wasn't. Guilty of leading him on…

But she wasn't doing that last, she tried to reassure herself. Neither of them was making any promises to the other. If anything, promises were exactly what the two of them were trying to avoid. And, truth be told, she still wasn't sure what her intentions were where Marcus was concerned. He was clearly interested in sharing more than champagne and an assortment of fruit and cheese with her. He was waiting for her to give him some sign that she was interested in more than that, too. And although there was a not-so-small part of her that was definitely interested, there was another part of her still clinging to rationality, to sanity, to fidelity.

Because even though succumbing to Marcus's seduction wouldn't make her unfaithful to another man, it would make her unfaithful to herself. She hadn't scrabbled her way out of the soul-swallowing slums and into one of Wall Street's most powerful, most dynamic investing firms by believing in fairy tales and capitulating to whimsy. She'd done it by being pragmatic, hardworking and focused.

Then again, being those things was also what had forced her to flee the very life she'd toiled in and fought so hard to build.

She sighed inwardly. There it was again. More

thinking about things she wasn't supposed to be thinking about tonight. Recalling the dissolution of her old life and fretting over the irresolution of her new one didn't belong in the fantasy life she was living *now.* It was her birthday. The one day of the year where it was okay for a person to be selfish and self-indulgent. It was the perfect time for her to be thinking about the moment. The moment was all that mattered for now. The moment was all she had that was certain. The moment was all she had that she could control. With another glance at Marcus—whose place in this night, in this moment, she still hadn't determined—she rose from her chair and moved to the French doors to watch the snow.

There was a small terrace beyond them, dark because of the late hour and frigid season. Della could just discern the outline of a handful of tables and chairs—all covered for the winter— and some potted topiaries that lay dormant. A layer of white covered all of it, so it must have been snowing harder and for longer than either of them had realized. Then again, when a woman was preoccupied by a man such as Marcus, it was hard to recognize that there was anything else out in the world at all.

As if conjured by the thought, she felt him slip up behind her, close enough that his body was flush against her own. She told herself she was only imagining the way she could feel the heat from his body mingling with hers, but the scent of him… That was all too real. All too wonderful. All too exhilarating.

"It was barely flurrying when I came in," she said. "I'm surprised how much has already fallen."

He said nothing for a moment, only continued to exude warmth and his intoxicatingly spicy fragrance. Finally, quietly, he said, "The snow isn't the only thing that's been surprising tonight."

She couldn't disagree. Yet as unexpected as Marcus had been, his presence somehow felt perfectly right. Prince Charming was the only thing that had been missing from Della's fairy-tale plan for the evening, even if he was a complete stranger. Then again, he wasn't a stranger, not really. They'd known each other for hours now. They'd shared, in a way, a lovely dinner, a spectacular opera, some quiet conversation and gentle touches. They'd made each other smile. They'd made each other laugh. They'd made each other…feel things.

Della liked Marcus. He liked her. That made them something more than strangers, surely. She just wasn't quite certain what.

Impulsively, she tested the handle of the door and found it unlocked. Another surprise. Or perhaps more magic. Unable to help herself, she pushed open the door and strode quickly out onto the terrace, turning around slowly in the falling snow.

"Della," Marcus objected from inside, "what are you doing? It's freezing out there."

Funny, but she didn't feel cold. On the contrary, being with him made her hot to her core.

"I can't help it," she said as she halted her rotation to face him. "It's so beautiful. And so quiet. Listen."

As happened with snow, the sounds of the city beyond the terrace were muffled and silent, but the snow itself seemed to make a soft, supple sound as it fell. Reluctantly, Marcus shoved his hands into his trouser pockets and walked onto the terrace, shaking his head at her.

"You're worse than a little kid," he said. But he was smiling that delicious smile again.

As he drew nearer, Della moved farther away, until she'd backed herself into the far corner of the terrace, away from the door. When her back bumped the wall, the motion unsettled a small bundle of snow from somewhere above her, sending it cascading down around over her. She laughed as she shook her head to scatter the flakes, then the comb that had been holding her hair came loose, making it fall around her shoulders. He came to her immediately, slipping a little on his way, grabbing the railing to steady himself as his laughter joined her own.

"Well, aren't we a mess?" she said.

Not that she cared. Her life had been a mess for a year now. At least this mess was a fun one. She extended her hand over the balcony to let the snowflakes collect in her palm one by one. As soon as they landed, they melted, but the moisture still sparkled against her skin. "Look at it, Marcus," she said. "How can you think it's not lovely?"

He tucked himself into the corner of the darkened terrace as snugly as she was. "It's cold," he corrected her. "And you left your coat inside."

As chivalrously as a paladin, he slipped off his tuxedo jacket and reached around her to drape it over her shoulders. The garment fairly swallowed her, but it was redolent with both his scent and his warmth, and she was helpless not to pull it more closely around herself.

"Now you'll get cold," she told him.

"I haven't been cold since the moment I laid eyes on you. A little thing like snow and subfreezing temperature isn't going to change that."

Della wasn't feeling cold, either. Not that that would make her return his jacket to him. It felt too nice being enveloped in it. Almost as if she were being enveloped by Marcus himself.

Almost.

As if reading her mind—again—he started to lean forward, dipping his head toward hers. Knowing he intended to kiss her, Della turned quickly away. Why, she had no idea. She wanted him to kiss her. She wanted to kiss him, too. But she still couldn't quite bring herself to allow it. She wasn't the woman he thought she was. She was beginning to wonder if she was even the woman *she* thought she was. Soon, she *would* be someone else—entirely and literally. And in a couple of hours, she and Marcus would be nothing but a fond memory lodged in each other's brains. What kind of memory did she want to be for him? What kind of memory did she want him to be for her?

Marcus didn't give her time to think about it, because the moment she had her back to him, he coiled both arms around her waist to pull her against himself. His broad chest more than spanned her shoulders, but his long torso aligned perfectly with hers. It was at the small of her back where she felt him most, however, because as he drew her closer, rubbing their bodies together, he stirred to life against her.

Della's heart rate quickened at the realization that he was becoming as aroused as she. Heat coursed through her when he dipped his head to hers, his mouth hovering just over her ear. His breath was warm and damp against her skin, at odds with the snow, clouding her senses until she was dizzy not knowing what was what.

"I can say the snow isn't lovely," he murmured, his voice as hot and demanding as the rest of him, "because I've seen something much lovelier this evening. In fact, you, my intriguing Della, are absolutely electrifying."

Instead of replying to that—mostly because she was afraid of what she might say…and even more afraid of what she might do—Della leaned further over the railing and into the falling snow. She turned her face to the caress of cold air, hoping it would be the antidote she needed to quell the swirling, simmering sensations inside her. Instead, her new position pushed her backside even more intimately against Marcus, and she felt him swell to even greater life against her.

She swallowed hard at the recognition of his condition, curling her fingers tightly over the metal railing, afraid of where her hands might wander otherwise. She wasn't so lucky with her thoughts, though, because they wandered plenty, telling her things she didn't want to hear. Things about how she would never meet another man like Marcus, and how he could be out of her life in a matter of moments, and how there was nothing sadder in life than a missed opportunity. So she tipped her face upward, welcoming the soft cascade of snowflakes, hoping they would numb her brain and make her forget…

…everything. Every ugly memory of where she'd grown up. Every miserable feeling she'd had since discovering the truth about Egan Collingwood. Every anxious moment she'd experienced since discovering even worse truths at work. Every terrible shudder of loneliness that had plagued her over the past eleven months. Every reason why she shouldn't do exactly what she wanted to do with Marcus. He was the surprise birthday gift that fate had presented her, sporting a big, satin bow.

Again, as if he'd read her mind, he covered her hands with his and gently urged them apart, opening his jacket over the front of her dress so that he could slip his fingers between the two garments. They went immediately to her rib cage, strumming it as if fine-tuning a delicate instrument. Ripples of pleasure wound through Della as he touched her, and she sighed her delight, her breath a puff of fog in the frigid air. Unable to help herself, she leaned against him, reaching behind herself with both hands to curl her fingers into his hair. Marcus used her new position to plunder her at will, covering her breasts with sure fingers.

"Oh," she murmured at his touch. "Oh, Marcus."

He said nothing in response, only dipped his head to her neck to drag kisses along the column of her throat. One hand gently kneaded her breast, while the other began to venture lower, moving along the elegant curves of her waist and hip and thigh, where he bunched the fabric of her dress in his fist. Slowly, slowly, oh…so slowly, he drew the garment upward, until Della could feel the cold and snow on her stocking-clad legs. Because of the gown's length, and because of the cold, she'd worn tights that rolled just above the knee, leaving her thighs bare. When she felt the whip of cold on her naked skin, she gasped, not only because of the frosty air, but also because she realized how far, how fast, things had progressed between them.

"Marcus," she began to protest. But the words sounded halfhearted, even to her own ears.

"Shh," he told her. "I just want to touch you. I just want to feel your skin beneath my fingertips."

She told herself to tell him he'd done that by holding her hand, but the words stilled before emerging. It had been so long since she'd felt a man's touch. Too long. She'd forgotten how delicious it felt to be this close to another human being. Had forgotten how essential it was to share physical intimacy with another person. Had forgotten how exquisite it could be, how alive it could make her feel. Had forgotten—

Marcus found the leg of her panties and pushed it aside, threading his fingers into the damp, molten core of her.

Oh...oh, Marcus... She'd forgotten how that could feel, too.

"You're so wet," he murmured against her ear, obviously surprised by her response to him.

"Della…oh, sweetheart…it's like… It's like you're already ready for me to—"

He moved his fingers against her again, eliciting a groan from deep inside her. Her fingers fell to the railing again, convulsing on it, then relaxed, then gripped the fixture again. Hard. She turned her fists first one way, then the other, then began to move them up and down along the length of the railing, the way she would touch a man's—

Marcus stroked her again, and somehow, she knew he was watching the movement of her hands and thinking the same thing she was thinking. Feeling the same thing she felt. Wanting the same thing she wanted.

He nuzzled her neck again, this time nipping her lightly with his teeth, an action she found unbelievably erotic. In response, she moved a hand behind herself and fumbled for his belt, working both it and the fly of his trousers open with trembling fingers.

Well, why shouldn't she? It was her birthday. She was celebrating. She'd already given herself so many gifts tonight. Why not one more? Why not enjoy this man the way they both wanted to enjoy each other?

When Marcus realized what she was doing, he moved away from her long enough to help her complete the action. She started to turn around, but he placed both hands firmly on her waist and held her in place with her back to him. So she reached behind herself and thrust her hand into his trousers, finding him naked and hard and ready. He gasped at what must have been the coldness of her hand, but she quickly warmed them both. Cupping the heavy head of his shaft in one hand, she palmed him over the satiny balm of his anticipated release before moving her fingers lower along his length. And lower. And lower. Until she caught her breath at just how magnificent he was.

She honestly wasn't sure what she had been thinking she would do next, and in that moment, Marcus's thoughts seemed to mirror her own. Dropping one hand from her waist, he fisted the fabric of her skirt again. Only this time, it was in the back, and this time he hiked it over her waist. As Della clung to the damp railing,

Marcus pulled down her panties, pushing them past her knees. Della did the rest, stepping completely out of them.

And then he was moving behind her again, deftly rolling on a condom he must have had at the ready. But then, he was notorious, wasn't he? She had only a scant second to marvel at how he was sexually indiscriminate enough to be so prepared for sex, yet responsible enough to take such a precaution. Then, as the snow cascaded around her, Marcus thrust himself into her from behind, burying himself deeply.

When she cried out at the depth of his penetration, he gently covered her mouth with his hand. Then he began to move inside her, pulling himself out almost completely before bucking against her again, going even deeper. She had to bite her lip to keep herself silent, but he rewarded her by moving his hand between her legs and fingering the damp folds of her flesh. Of course, that only made her want to cry out again…

But she didn't cry out. She only felt. Felt the tight coil of heat in her belly pull tighter still, until her entire body seemed ready to explode. She felt the man behind her fill her again and again and again, felt the dizzying sensations of hunger and desire and need mingling and twining until they all became one. And then she felt the white-hot release of her climax shaking her, followed immediately by his.

And then he was removing himself from inside her and wrapping up the spent condom, rearranging their clothes as best he could before he spun her around and covered her mouth with his. For a long time, he only kissed her and kissed her and kissed her. Then, finally, he pulled back enough so that he could frame her face with both hands. It was snowing harder now, swirls of powder blowing up onto the terrace, surrounding them in a virtual tornado of white. Marcus's breath was coming in gasps, puffs of white against the sparkle of snow that merged with her own hitched breathing.

He dipped his head until his forehead was pressed against hers. "Nothing like that has ever happened to me before," he said between breaths. "Della, my God. You're a narcotic."

She wasn't sure how to reply to that, so she said nothing. She only curled her fingers in the front of his shirt and clung to him. They stood that way for long moments, neither seeming to know what to say or do. Della was confident no one inside the club had seen what had happened. Not only was the place deserted by now, but the two of them had also been obscured by both the darkness and the blowing snow. She also noted with a smile that they'd managed to fog up the windows behind them to opacity.

Finally, Marcus pulled away from her. But only far enough that he could gaze into her face. She'd expected him to demand the return of his jacket and say something like, "Holy cow, would you look at the time? I gotta get outta here."

Instead, he threaded his fingers gently into her hair and, very softly, asked, "Do you know what my favorite thing is about the Windsor Club?"

Still not trusting her voice, Della only shook her head.

"My favorite thing is that it's connected to the Ambassador Hotel. On nights like this, when driving could be dangerous due to a mix of weather, darkness and extremely good champagne, you can just…spend the night there. You don't have to set foot outside to get there. You can walk down the hall and through a breezeway and be at the registration desk in a matter of minutes. And, thanks to your platinum club status, within minutes of that, you can be in a luxury suite ordering another bottle of champagne from their twenty-four-hour room service."

Finally finding her voice, Della told him, "But I don't have platinum club status at the Ambassador Hotel."

He feigned forgetfulness. "That's right. You just came to Chicago recently, didn't you? So I guess you'll have to be with someone else who has platinum club status."

She smiled. "And who could I possibly know who might have that?"

"So it wouldn't be a problem for you spending the night at the Ambassador? With me? You don't have any…obligations waiting for you anywhere?"

Only the obligation of returning her clothes by

noon and checking in with Geoffrey by nine, as she did every morning. And she always woke by five, even without an alarm, even after a sleepless night. It was ingrained in her because Mr. Nathanson, her boss, had always insisted she be at her desk the same time he was—at 7:00 a.m. sharp, before anyone else showed up for work. At the time, Della had thought it was because the man was a workaholic. Had she known it was actually because he was corrupt…

She turned her attention to Marcus again, where it belonged. He was a gift, she reminded herself. One night with him would be the most amazing birthday present she'd ever received— from herself to herself. It would be terrible not to accept a gift like him.

"No," she finally said. "I don't have any… obligations." She lifted a hand to thread her fingers through his hair, loving the way the snow had dampened it and their encounter had warmed it. "Not until tomorrow. One night, Marcus," she made herself say, because it was very, very important that he realize that was all it would be. It was even more important that she realize it. "One night is all I can promise you."

"One night is all I'm asking for, Della."

It was probably all he wanted from any woman, she thought. Because it was probably all a man like him could promise in return.

She told herself that made her feel better. They both wanted the same thing. They both needed the same thing. They were both willing to give and take equally. Tonight would be exactly what she had planned it to be all those years ago: One night. Of magic. Her gift to herself.

Marcus lifted his hand to trace a finger lightly over her cheek. "Well, then, my sweet, intriguing Della," he said softly, "why don't you and I take a little walk and find out where it leads?"

Four

Marcus stood at the broad window of the hotel suite dressed in the plush royal blue robe the hotel so thoughtfully provided for all its guests and watched the snow fall. And fall. And fall. And fall. Fat, furious flakes coming down so thick and so fast, he could barely make out the buildings on the other side of Michigan Avenue.

Unbelievable. What was supposed to have been a manageable snowfall of three to five inches had turned into a blizzard during the night. The entire city was on hold until the snowplows could get out and do their thing, but since everyone had been caught by surprise, they couldn't do anything until the snow let up. A lot.

And the snow didn't show any sign of letting up. At all.

The situation was going to be untenable for a while. No one would be going anywhere until tomorrow at the earliest. Not that Marcus cared. Because it meant that the one night Della had promised was all she could give him would now, by necessity, become two.

That was something he should definitely care about. The last thing he looked for in a one-night stand was for it to last more than one night. Hell, half the time he was safely back at his place before the night was even over. Once he was sexually satisfied by a woman, there was never any reason to hang around. Even the prospect of being sexually satisfied a second time rarely kept him from leaving.

But with Della, even being satisfied a third time hadn't quelled his appetite for more. Once he'd regained enough strength to manage it. They'd both been insatiable last night, to the point where they'd slept only long enough to recover from their previous coupling, then come together even more fiercely than before. That third time, they'd had to rely on oral gratification alone to bring each other to climax, since the second time had been so rough. Not that either of them had seemed to mind. Della had been as demanding and wild as a tigress, and Marcus had mounted her the way a jungle cat would have claimed his mate.

And even that hadn't been enough to satisfy him. In fact, that had only made him want her more. When he'd awoken that morning beside her, their bodies had been so intricately entwined, he'd barely been able to tell where hers ended and his began. Marcus never slept with a woman after having sex with her. Never. And he'd certainly never gathered one close that way and held her with such possessiveness. For a long time after waking, he'd only lain silently beside her, holding her, listening to her soft respiration, inhaling her scent. It was different now. Last night she'd smelled soft and flowery. This morning she smelled musky and dark. And, God help him, Marcus had grown hard against her as he lay there, and it had been all he could do not to take her again in her sleep. Instead, he'd eased his way out of the bed without waking her, donned the robe and called for room service.

Even its arrival hadn't woken Della. But that might be because Marcus had intercepted the steward in the hallway when he'd heard the rattle of the approaching cart and brought it in himself. He hadn't wanted to wake her before she was ready. Strangely, however, that hadn't been because he wanted her rested up for another night like last night—and, hey, maybe a day like last night, too—but because he simply liked watching her sleep.

He turned away from the window and let go of the sheer curtains, throwing the room into an otherworldly dusk created by the thickly falling snow. He loved the understated luxury of the Ambassador, loved the taupe walls and buff-colored, cleanly tailored furnishings with the dashes of blues and greens in the form of throw pillows and abstract artwork. He'd wanted a suite, of course, but there hadn't been one available. At the time, it hadn't seemed a problem, since he'd known he and Della would only need the place for a few hours. Now that their stay was looking to be for most of the weekend, it would have been nice to have a little more room to spread out.

He looked over at the bed, where she still slept, and smiled. Then again, there was a lot to be said for close quarters. Even if those quarters were still five-star hotel roomy.

Della lay on her stomach, the ivory sheets tangled over her lower half, her creamy back and shoulders laid bare. Silently, he neared the bed, pausing beside it. Her hair flowed like a honey river above her head and down the side of the pillow, and her hand was curled into a loose fist near her mouth. Her lips were swollen from the ferocity of their kisses, and her cheek was pink where his beard had abraded her. He remembered wrapping fistfuls of that hair around his fingers as he'd ridden her last night, then stroking it back into place as the two of them had gentled their movements in the afterglow. Even in the furiousness of their actions, he'd noted how thick and silky the strands were, and he'd loved the feel of her soft tresses tumbling through his fingers.

He was about to turn away to pour two cups of coffee—maybe the aroma of Jamaica Blue Mountain would rouse her—when she began to stir. Slowly, murmuring soft sounds of wakefulness, she inhaled a deep, satisfied breath and released it slowly. Her eyes still closed, she rolled over and arched her arms over her head for an idle stretch. The action displayed her full breasts to their best advantage, stiffening her rosy nipples. Then she straightened her legs to stretch them, too, the sheet falling away as she spread them open, making visible the dark blond nest between her legs.

Again, Marcus stirred to life simply looking at her. She was utter perfection, beauty so unflawed and pure that he almost wished he hadn't sullied her.

Almost.

Instead, unable to help himself, he leaned over and traced the pad of his middle finger along her calf.

She moaned softly in response to his touch,

smiling a very tempting smile, but she still didn't open her eyes. So Marcus drew his finger higher, up over her knee and along her thigh. She gasped a little this time, then uttered a low, erotic sound that seemed to come from deep inside her. But she still didn't open her eyes.

So Marcus leaned over the bed, moving his finger to the inside of her thigh, closer to the juncture of her legs. Della, in turn, opened her legs wider. Now Marcus smiled, too, and drove his hand into the silky thatch of curls hiding the feminine core of her. For long seconds, he furrowed her with light, slow, measured movements, pushing his fingers through the hot, damp folds of flesh. Deliberately, he avoided the sweet little spot that would drive her over the edge, but he skirted close a time or two, just to hear her swift intake of breath and ensuing groan of pleasure. When he pulled away again, he slipped a finger inside her, gently, since he knew she must still be tender from the night before. When she lifted her hips from the mattress to pull him deeper, he withdrew his finger, then inserted it slowly again. And again. And again.

When he knew she was at the verge of coming apart, he brought his thumb into the action, this time settling it resolutely on her now-drenched skin. It was easy for him to rub the pad of his thumb over her sweet spot, even when she began bucking her hips wildly at the onslaught. His fingers were covered with her essence now, making his manipulations come more quickly, more insistently. With one final push, he brought her to climax, making her cry out at the sensations that rocked her. She arched one last time, then slowly came back down to the bed. Marcus drew his hand up along her naked torso, leaving a trail of her own satisfaction in his wake, circling first one nipple, then the other, before moving his hand to the delicate lines of her neck.

"Good morning," he said softly, as if the last few minutes hadn't happened.

She was still breathing raggedly and trembling from his touch, but she managed to whisper, "Oh, yes. It is a *very* good morning. I could wake up that way every morning."

The words should have had panic racing through Marcus. The last thing he wanted to hear was a woman including him in her everyday life. Instead, he found himself warming to the idea of waking her that way each day. Doubtless because any man who started his day knowing he'd brought a woman to climax took with him a sense of power and well-being. Not to mention smugness. It made a man feel as if he could do just about anything.

It had nothing to do with simply enjoying an intimate moment with an exceptional woman.

"There's coffee," he said. "And breakfast. I didn't know what you'd like, so I ordered some of everything."

"Coffee," she said, still a little breathless. "Black," she added as he was about to ask how she took it—almost as if she were reading his mind.

That, too, should have made him bristle. He didn't want women understanding the workings of his brain. Mostly because few of them would approve of his thoughts, since they generally consisted of: A) women other than the one he was with, B) work, C) women other than the one he was with, D) how well the Cubs, Bears or Blackhawks were performing, depending on the season or E) women other than the one he was with.

But he kind of liked the connection with Della and, strangely, didn't want to think of anyone or anything other than her. So he only said, "Coming right up."

By the time he finished pouring two cups and removing the lids from the cold dishes the steward had brought up, Della was out of bed and wrapped in a robe identical to his own—except that hers swallowed her—and was standing at the window the same way he had been earlier. The snow was still coming down as opaquely as it had been then, and he thought he saw her shake her head.

"It's like a blizzard out there," she murmured incredulously.

"No, it *is* a blizzard out there," Marcus corrected as he came to a halt beside her and extended a cup of coffee, black like his own, toward her.

She took it automatically with one hand, still

holding open the curtain with the other. "How are we going to get…home?"

He noted her hesitation on the last word, as if home for her were a somewhat tentative state. Another clue that she really was only visiting here. Nevertheless, she'd assured Marcus that no one would miss her—at least not until today. Both thoughts bothered him a lot more than they should. For one thing, it shouldn't matter if Della was tied to another man, since Marcus didn't want to stake a claim on her anyway. For another thing, they'd both only wanted and promised one night, that should have been more than enough to satisfy their desire to enjoy each other for a little while. The fact that she was only in Chicago temporarily or might be involved with someone else should be of no consequence. In fact, it should reassure him that there would indeed be no strings attached.

For some reason, though, Marcus didn't like the idea of her being only a visitor to Chicago. He liked even less that she might be involved with someone else.

Too much thinking, he told himself, and way

too early in the day for it. It was the weekend. He was snowbound with a gorgeous, incredibly sexy woman. Why was he thinking at all?

"No one is going anywhere today," he said before sipping his coffee. "Not even the snow-plows will be able to get out until this lets up."

Della turned to look at him, and that strange, panicked look he'd seen for a few moments last night was back in her eyes. "But I can't stay here all day," she told him, the panic present in her voice now, too. "I have to get…home."

Again the hesitation before the final word, he noted. Again, he didn't like it.

"Is there someplace you absolutely have to be today?" When she didn't reply right away, only arrowed her eyebrows in even more concern, he amended, "Or should I ask, is there some*one* who's expecting you to be someplace today?"

She dropped her gaze at that. Pretty much the only reaction he needed. So there was indeed someone else in her life. Someone she'd have to answer to for any kind of prolonged absence.

"Is it a husband?" he asked, amazed at how

casual the question sounded, when he was suddenly feeling anything but.

Her gaze snapped up to his, flashing with anger. Good. Anger was better than panic. Anger stemmed from passion, not fear. "I wouldn't be here with you if I had a husband waiting for me."

Marcus had no idea why he liked that answer so much.

"What about you?" she countered. "Is there a wife somewhere waiting for you? Or has she come to expect this kind of behavior from you?"

He chuckled at that. "The day I have a wife waiting for me somewhere is the day they put me in a padded cell." When she still didn't seem satisfied by the answer—he couldn't imagine why not—he told her bluntly, "I'm not married, Della." Not sure why he bothered to add it, he said, "There's no one waiting anywhere for me." Then, after only a small hesitation, he added, "But there is someone who will be worried about you if you don't come…home…today, isn't there?" He deliberately paused before the word *home,* too, to let her know he'd noticed her own hesitation.

She inhaled a deep breath and released it slowly, then dropped the curtain and curled both hands around the white china coffee cup. She gazed into its depths instead of at Marcus when she spoke. "Home is something of a fluid concept for me at the moment."

Fluid. Interesting word choice. "And by that you mean…?"

Still staring at her coffee, she said, "I can't really explain it to you."

"Can't or won't?"

Now she did meet his gaze. But her expression was void of anything. No panic, no anger, nothing. "Both."

"Why?"

She only shook her head. She brought the cup to her mouth, blew softly on its surface and enjoyed a careful sip. Then she strode to the breakfast cart to inspect its choices. But he couldn't help noting how she looked at the clock as she went, or how her eyes went wide in surprise when she saw the time. It wasn't even eight o'clock yet. On a Sunday, no less. It seemed too early for anyone to have missed her if she had been able to surrender an entire night.

"You really did order a little of everything," she said as she began lifting lids. "Pastries, bacon, sausage, eggs, fruit…"

He thought about saying something about how they both needed to regain their strength after last night, but for some reason, it felt crass to make a comment like that. Another strange turn of events, since Marcus had never worried about being crass before. Besides, what else was there for the two of them to talk about after the kind of night they'd had? Their response to each other had been sexual from the get-go. They'd barely exchanged a dozen words between the time they left the club and awoke this morning—save the earthy, arousing ones they'd uttered about what they wanted done and were going to do to each other. Ninety percent of their time together had been spent copulating. Nine percent had been spent flirting and making known the fact that they wanted to copulate. What were they supposed to say to each other that didn't involve sex? Other than, how do you take your coffee or what did you think of *La Bohème?* And they'd already covered both.

She plucked a sticky pastry from the pile and set it on one of the empty plates. Then, after a small pause, she added another. Then a third. Then she added some strawberries and a couple of slices of cantaloupe. Guess she, too, thought they needed to rebuild their strength after the night they'd had. But, like him, she didn't want to say it out loud.

"Sweet tooth, huh?" he asked as she licked a bit of frosting from the pad of her thumb.

"Just a little," she agreed. Balancing both the plate and cup, she moved to the bed and set them on the nightstand beside it. Then she climbed into bed.

Well, that was certainly promising.

Marcus filled the other plate with eggs, bacon and a bagel, then retrieved his coffee and joined her, placing his breakfast on the opposite nightstand. Where she had seated herself with her legs crossed pretzel-fashion facing him, he leaned against the headboard with his legs extended before him. Noting the way her robe gaped open enough to reveal the upper swells of her breasts, it occurred to him that neither of them had a stitch of clothing to wear except for last night's evening attire, that wasn't exactly the kind of thing a person wanted to wear during the day when a person was trying to make him- or herself comfortable.

Oh, well.

He watched her nibble a strawberry and wondered how he could find such an innocent action so arousing. Then he wondered why he was even asking himself that. Della could make changing a tire arousing.

"Well, since you won't tell me why home is so fluid," he said, "will you at least tell me where you're making it at the moment?"

"No," she replied immediately.

He thought about pressing her on the matter, then decided to try a different tack. "Then will you tell me what brings you to Chicago?"

"No," she responded as quickly.

He tried again. "Will you tell me where you're from originally?"

"No."

"How long you're going to be here?"

"No."

"Where you're going next?"

"No."

"How old you are?"

"Certainly not."

"Do you like piña coladas and getting caught in the rain?"

He wasn't sure, but he thought she may have smiled at that. "Not particularly."

"How about fuzzy gray kittens, volunteering for public television, long walks on the beach, cuddling by firelight and the novels of Philip Roth?"

At that, she only arrowed her eyebrows down in confusion.

"Oh, right. Sorry. That was Miss November. My bad."

Her expression cleared, but she said nothing.

"What's your sign?" Marcus tried again.

That, finally, did make her smile. It wasn't a big smile, but it wasn't bad. It was something they could work on.

"Sagittarius," she told him.

Now that said a lot about her, Marcus thought. Or, at least, it would. If he knew a damned thing about astrology. Still, it was something. Sagittariuses were born in June, weren't they? Or was it October? March?

All right, all right. So he knew as much about her now as he had when he started his interrogation. Which was nothing. Hell, he didn't even know if she was telling the truth about being a Sagittarius or not liking piña coladas and getting caught in the rain.

Immediately, however, he knew she was telling the truth about those things. He had no idea why, but he was confident Della wasn't a liar. She was just a woman who wouldn't reveal anything meaningful about herself and who was sneaking around on a lover. Had she been a liar, she would have had a phony answer for every question he asked, and she would have painted herself as someone she wasn't. Instead, he was left with a blank slate of a woman who could be anyone.

But that, too, wasn't right, he thought. There were a lot of things he knew about Della. He knew she loved an esoteric art form that most people her age had never even tried to expose themselves to. He knew she cried at all the sad parts of an opera, and that she was awed by the intricacies of the music. He'd seen all those reactions on her face when he'd watched her last night instead of *La Bohème*. He knew she liked champagne. He knew she was enchanted by a snowfall. He knew she laughed easily. He knew she was comfortable in red, red, red. All of those things spoke volumes about a person.

And he knew she came from a moneyed background, even if she was currently making her way by having someone else pay for it. It hadn't taken an inspection of her jewelry or a look at the labels in her clothing—even though he had as he'd picked up their things from the floor while she slept—to know that. She was smart, confident and articulate, and had clearly been educated at excellent schools. She carried herself with sophistication and elegance, obviously having been raised by parents for whom such things were important. She'd been perfectly at ease last night in every venue he'd encountered her. If she wasn't the product of wealth and refinement, Marcus was a bloated yak.

Not that wealth and refinement necessarily manufactured a product that was all the things Della was. He need only point to himself to prove that. He'd been kicked out of every tony private school his parents had enrolled him in, until his father finally bought off the director of the last one with a massive contribution for the construction of a new multimedia center. The same contribution had bought Marcus's diploma, since his grades hadn't come close to winning him that. Not because he hadn't been smart, but because he hadn't given a damn. As for sophistication and elegance, he had gone out of his way as a teenager to be neither and had embarrassed his family at every society function he'd attended. He'd raided liquor cabinets, ransacked cars and ruined debutantes—often in the same evening—and he'd earned an arrest record before he even turned sixteen. If it hadn't had been for Charlotte…

He pushed the memories away and instead focused on Della. If it hadn't had been for Charlotte, Marcus wouldn't be sitting here with her right now. And not only because Charlotte's absence last night had allowed him to strike up a conversation with Della, not once, but three times. But because if it hadn't had been for Charlotte, Marcus would now either be in a minimum security prison for wreaking havoc and general mischief past the age of eighteen, or he'd be lolling about on skid row, having been finally disowned by his family.

"What are you thinking about?"

Della's question brought him completely to the present. But it wasn't a question he wanted to answer. Hey, why should he, when she wouldn't answer any of his?

At his silence, she added, "You looked so far away there for a minute."

"I was far away."

"Where?"

He sipped his coffee and met her gaze levelly. "I'm not telling."

"Why not?"

"You won't tell me anything about you, so I'm not telling you anything about me."

For a minute, he thought maybe she'd back-pedal and offer up some answers to his questions in order to get answers to some of her own. Instead, she nodded and said, "It's for the best that way."

Damn. So much for reverse psychology.

"For you or for me?" he asked.

"For both of us."

The more she said, the more puzzled and curious Marcus grew. Just who the hell was she? Where had she come from? Where was she going? Why wouldn't she tell him anything about herself? And why, dammit, did he want so desperately to know everything there was to know about her?

"All right, if you really want to know, I was thinking about something at work," he lied.

She said nothing in response, only picked up one of the pastries and enjoyed a healthy bite.

"Don't you want to at least know what I do for a living?"

"No."

There was that word again. He was really beginning to hate it.

"I work for a brokerage house," he told her, deliberately being vague about his position there, since he still wasn't sure how much to say. Actually, that wasn't quite true. He wanted to say a lot about himself. But not for the usual reasons. Usually, he only opened up to a woman by saying things designed to impress her, in order to get her more quickly into bed. But he'd already gotten Della into bed and still wanted to impress her. That was strange enough in itself. Even stranger was how he suspected that the best way to impress her was to *not* brag about himself. Well, not just yet, anyway.

She was swallowing when he told her about his job, but it must have gone down the wrong way, because she immediately began to cough. A lot. Marcus was about to reach over to pat her on the back—or administer the Heimlich if necessary—but she held up a hand to stop him and reached for her coffee instead. After a couple of sips, she was okay. Though her face still looked a little pale.

"I'm fine," she said before he could ask. "That swallow went down the wrong way."

He nodded. And once he knew she really was fine, he picked up the conversation where he'd left off. "I work at—"

"Stop," she said, holding up a hand as if trying to physically stop the information from coming. "Don't tell me what you do or where you work. Please, Marcus. We agreed. No background information. No last names. No strings. No past, no present, no future."

"We also agreed only one night, " he reminded her, "but that's obviously not going to be the case. We're stuck here for at least another twenty-four hours. There's no harm in getting to know each other a little better. Unless you can tell me one."

He could see by her expression she could think of at least one. Maybe two. Maybe ten. Never in his life had he met a woman whose face was such an open book. Forget mind reading. A man could discover a lot about Della just by looking at her face. And what Marcus discovered now was that there was no way she was going to open up about herself to him.

Still, that didn't mean he couldn't open himself up to her.

"I work at Fallon Brothers," he said before she could stop him. He didn't add that the Fallons in the name of the multibillion-dollar company that employed him were his great-great grandfather and great-great uncle or that he was the fourth generation of the Fallon empire that would someday be running the company, along with his cousin Jonathan. Except that Marcus was the one who would become CEO upon his father's retirement next year, that meant he would be doing even less work than he was now as a VP, and then the partying would *really* begin. If Marcus was a fixture of the tabloid rags and websites now, he intended to be a permanent, cemented, superglued fixture once he didn't have to answer to his father anymore.

"Marcus, please," Della said again, her voice laced with warning. "Don't say another—"

"My permanent residence is on Lakeshore Drive," he continued, ignoring her. He picked up the pad and pen labeled with the hotel's logo that lay on the nightstand near his breakfast. "Here. I'll write it down for you," he continued, and proceeded to do just that. "But I also have places in London, Hong Kong, Tokyo and Aruba. All the big financial capitals, in fact."

When he looked up after finishing the last digit of his cell number—he'd given her the numbers of the office and his penthouse, too—she was gazing at him with much consternation.

Damn, she was cute when she was consternated.

"Since when is Aruba a big financial capital?" she asked.

"Since I spent a fortune on a house there and spend another fortune on rum every time I go down there."

"I see."

"I'm thirty-eight years old and a Chicago native," he added as he dropped the pad with his address and phone numbers onto the mattress between them. Not that Della even glanced at them. "As an undergrad, I majored in business at Stanford, then got my MBA from Harvard. Yes, I am that clichéd businessman you always hear about, except that I didn't graduate anywhere near the top of my class either time. Doesn't mean I'm not good at what I do," he hastened to add, "it just means I'm not an overachiever—that's where the cliché ends—and that I make time for more than work." He threw her his most lascivious look, just in case she didn't get that part. Which he was pretty sure she did, because she blushed that becoming shade of pink she had last night.

"Marcus, I really wish you wouldn't—"

"Let's see, what else is worth mentioning?" he interrupted, ignoring her. "I broke my arm in a skiing accident when I was eight and broke my ankle in a riding accident when I was ten. I have two sisters—both older and married to men my parents chose for them…not that either of them would ever admit that—along with two nieces and three nephews. My favorite color is red." He hoped she got the significance of that, too, and was more than a little delighted when color bloomed on her cheeks again. "My favorite food is Mediterranean in general and Greek in particular. I usually drive a black Bentley, but I also have a vintage Jaguar roadster—it goes without saying that it's British racing green—and a red Maserati. You already know about the opera thing, but my second greatest passion is port wine. My sign is Leo. And," he finally concluded, "I don't like piña coladas or getting caught in the rain, either."

By the time he finished, Della's irritation at him was an almost palpable thing. He'd sensed it growing as he'd spoken, until he'd halfway expected her to cover her ears with her hands and start humming, then say something like, "La la la la la. I can't hear you. I have my fingers in my ears and I'm humming. La la la la la."

Instead, she'd spent the time nervously breaking her pastry into little pieces and dropping them onto her plate. Now that he was finished, she shifted her gaze from his to those little broken pieces and said, "I really wish you hadn't told me those things."

"Why not?"

"Because every time I discover something else about you, it makes you that much more difficult to forget."

Something stirred to life inside him at her words, but he couldn't say exactly what that something was. It wasn't an unpleasant sensation, but neither was it exactly agreeable. It was just…different. Something he'd never felt before. Something it would take some time to explore.

"That's interesting," he told her. "Because I don't know one tenth that much about you, and I know you're going to be impossible to forget."

Still studying the broken pastry, she made a face, as if she hadn't realized what a mess she'd made of it. She placed the plate on the mattress on top of the pad of paper with the information he'd written down, though he was pretty sure she'd given it a quick glance before covering it. With any luck, she had a photographic memory. With even more luck, he'd notice later that the slip of paper had moved from the bed into her purse.

Her purse, he thought. Women's purses were notorious for storing information—probably more than a computer's hard drive. Not that Marcus could vouch for such a thing. He'd never had the inclination to search a woman's purse before. It was actually a pretty despicable thing for a man to even consider doing.

He couldn't wait to get into Della's.

"All right," she said. "I'll tell you a few things about myself."

Finally, they were getting somewhere. Just where, exactly, he wasn't sure he could say. But it was farther down the road than they'd been a few minutes ago. He wished he could see farther still, to find out if the road was a long and winding one with hills and valleys and magnificent vistas, or if it ended abruptly in a dead end where a bridge had washed out, and where there were burning flares and warning sirens and pylons strung with yellow tape that read Caution!

Then again, did he really care? It wasn't as if anything as minor as cataclysmic disaster had ever stopped him from going after what he wanted before. And he did want Della. He wanted her a lot.

Five

Della tried not to notice how Marcus seemed to have moved closer to her during their exchange. She couldn't help noting other things, however. Such as how love-tousled his dark hair was and how the shadow of beard covered the lower half of his face, both qualities evoking an air of danger about him. Or maybe it was just that she realized now how very dangerous he was. How dangerous her behavior last night had been. How dangerous it was to still be with him this morning with no way to get home. Not only because she was at greater risk of Geoffrey discovering her absence, but also because she was beginning to feel things for Marcus that she had no business feeling. Things that would make it more difficult to leave him when the time came.

She never, ever, should have allowed herself to succumb to her desires last night. Hadn't she learned the hard way how doing that led to trouble? The last time she'd yielded so easily to a man, her life had been left in a shambles. And Egan had been nowhere near as compelling or unforgettable as Marcus.

"I'm originally from the East Coast," she said, hoping that small snippet of information—even if it was a hugely broad one that could mean anything—would appease him.

She should have known better.

"Where on the east coast?" he asked.

She frowned at him and repeated stubbornly, "The east coast."

"North or south?"

"That's all I'm giving you, Marcus. Don't push or that's the only thing you'll learn about me."

He opened his mouth to say more, then shut it again. He was probably recalling how she'd told him she came from someplace hot, and he was assuming it was the latter. But he was clearly not happy about having to acquiesce to her demand.

She wasn't sure whether or not to confess anything about her family, mostly because she hadn't seen any of them for years. Even when they'd all lived under one roof, they hadn't really been much of a family. It was a sad thing to admit, but Della really didn't have feelings for any of them one way or another. Still, if Marcus wanted information, maybe that would be the kind to give him because it wouldn't cost her anything emotionally. It would also potentially be misleading, since most people stayed in touch with their blood relations, so he might think she hadn't traveled too far from her own.

"I have an older brother," she admitted. "And a younger brother, as well." The first had taken off when he was sixteen and Della was four-teen, and she hadn't seen him since. The other, last time she'd heard—which had been about ten years ago—had joined a gang. At the tender age of fifteen. No telling where he was now, either.

On the few occasions when Della thought about her brothers, she tried to convince herself that they'd been motivated by the same things she had, and in the same way. She told herself they'd gotten out of the old neighborhood and found better lives, just as she had. Sometimes she even believed herself. But more often, she feared they had screwed up everything in their lives, too, the same way she had.

"Nieces and nephews?" Marcus asked.

She only shook her head in response to that. To her, the gesture meant *I don't know.* To Marcus, let it mean whatever he wanted it to.

"Any injuries sustained as a child?" he asked, referring to his own.

She supposed she could tell him about the time she cut her foot on a broken beer bottle in a vacant lot during a game of stickball and had to get stitches, but that didn't quite compare to skiing and riding accidents. So she only said, "None worth mentioning."

"Schooling?" he asked.

The School of Hard Knocks, she wanted to say. It was either that, or her infamously crime-ridden high school or disgracefully underachieving elementary school. But neither of those would be the answer he was looking for.

Della knew he was looking for specific answers. He wanted her to be a specific kind of woman. The kind of woman who came from the same society he did and who lived and moved there as easily as he. She wasn't sure if he was the sort of blue blood who would turn his nose up in disgust at her if he knew her true origins, but he would, without question, be disappointed. She was glamorous to him. He'd made that clear. She was intriguing. A woman of mystery and erotica. The last thing he wanted to hear her say was that she'd grown up in a slum, had no formal education, had clawed and fought to win every scrap she ever had, and had taught herself everything she knew by emulating others.

So she said, "Yes. I had schooling."

He smiled at that. "No. I meant where did you go to—"

"My favorite color is blue," she told him. "And my favorite food is *fruits de mer.*" Her French, she was proud to say, sounded as good as his Italian had last night. Unfortunately, *fruits de mer* was about the only thing she could say in French, and only because she'd practiced it for her menu lesson.

"After opera," she continued, "my greatest passion is—"

She halted abruptly. Now here was a problem. Because other than opera, Della really had no passions. She'd never really had an opportunity to find any. After landing the job at Whitworth and Stone when she was eighteen, she'd focused entirely on it in order to stay employed there. She'd worked overtime whenever she could for the money, and she'd spent the rest of her time trying to better herself in whatever ways she could. Reading classic novels from the library. Emulating the speech of actors in movies. Swiping magazines she found in the apartment's recycling bin to educate herself about fashion and etiquette and how to act like a refined human being. Opera had been the only indulgence she'd allowed herself, both because she loved it and it contributed to the kind of person she wanted to be. Beyond that…

Beyond that, she'd never had much of anything else to love.

"After opera…" Marcus prodded her now.

She looked at him, biting back another surge of panic. Never had she felt like a greater impostor than she did in that moment. She really did have nothing. Not a thing in the world. For the first time since leaving her life—such as it was—in New York, she realized how utterly empty her life had been and how absolutely alone she was.

"After opera…" She felt the prickle of tears sting her eyes. No, please. Anything but that. Not here. Not now. Not in front of Marcus. She hadn't cried since she was a child. Not once. Not when things had fallen apart in New York. Not when Geoffrey had told her she had to leave with him. Not during the eleven months since, when she'd had to turn her entire life over to someone else. Why now? Why here? Why in front of the last person on earth she wanted to see her cry?

She lifted a hand to shield her face and jumped up from the bed. "Excuse me," she said hastily as she headed for the bathroom. "I think I have an eyelash in my eye." As she was closing the door, she said over her shoulder, "If you don't mind, I'll take the first shower." Without awaiting a reply, she pushed the door closed and locked it, then turned on the shower full blast. Then she grabbed a towel and dropped to the floor, shoving it hard against her mouth.

I will not cry. I will not cry. I will not cry. I will not cry.

Her eyes grew damp, so she squeezed them shut.

I will not cry. I will not cry. I will not cry. I will not cry.

And somehow, by some miracle, Della kept the tears at bay.

The moment Marcus heard the rattle of the shower curtain closing in the bathroom, he crossed to the dresser where Della had laid her purse the night before. Okay, so maybe this one couldn't hold as much as a computer's hard drive, since it was one of those tiny purses women carried to formal events that was roughly the size of a negative ion. But it was large enough to hold a driver's license, cash and a cell phone, all of which he found inside, along with a tube of lipstick, a collapsible hairbrush, a plain metal keychain from which dangled a single key—house key, not car key—and, curiously, a computer USB drive. But no credit card, he noted, thinking it odd. Meaning she'd paid for her dinner and whatever else last night—a not inconsiderable sum—with cash. Interesting. He just wasn't sure exactly how.

He looked at the driver's license first and saw that it was from New York State. So she had been honest with him about being from the East Coast, but hadn't dissuaded him of his assumption that she came from a hot climate. Also interesting. But again, he wasn't sure how. Looking closer at the license, he saw that her full name was Della Louise Hannan and that she was thirty years old. In fact, she'd turned thirty yesterday. So last night was her celebration of reaching that milestone. The fact that she'd celebrated it alone heartened him—more than it really should have.

He glanced at her address, but it was on one of the higher numbered streets, outside the part of Manhattan with which he was familiar. He knew the better parts of New York like the back of his hand and had expected he would be able to pinpoint Della's address with little effort—doubtless somewhere near or on Fifth Avenue or Central Park. But this was nowhere close to either of those. He memorized it for future investigation, stuck the license in her purse and withdrew her cell phone, flipping it open.

Unfortunately, it was one of those not-particularly-smart phones, a bare-bones model that didn't contain an easy-access menu. So he had to poke around a bit to find what he was looking for, namely her calls received and sent. After a moment, he found both and discovered that every single one had been to and from one person. A person identified simply as Geoffrey.

Any optimism Marcus had begun to feel dissolved at that. Geoffrey could be a first or last name, but somehow he knew that it was definitely a man's name. He fumbled through more screens until he found her contact list and began to scroll to *G*. It took a while to get there. She had dozens of contacts, most listed by last name, but a handful—mostly women—were identified by their first names and, when the names were duplicates, by a last initial. Finally, he came to Geoffrey and clicked on it. There were two numbers listed for him, one designated a work number, the other a cell. The work number was a three one two area code—the man worked in Chicago. The cell number, however, was eight four seven, that was in the suburbs. It was a revelation that revealed nothing to Marcus. A lot of people lived in the 'burbs and worked in the city. And eight four seven covered a lot of 'burbs.

He reminded himself that Geoffrey could be a brother or a cousin or some guy she knew from high school. There was no reason to think he was necessarily a love interest or the man who kept her. Except for the fact that he was clearly the only person she was in touch with, in spite of her knowing a lot more.

But that was what men like that did, didn't they? They isolated the woman they wanted to own from her friends and family until she had no one but the guy to rely on. Whoever this Geoffrey was, Marcus was liking him less and less.

That was saying something, because Marcus had begun to really loathe the faceless, name-less man in Della's life without even knowing for sure one existed.

He scrolled through more screens until he found the one that contained her photographs and clicked on those. There weren't a lot, but there were enough to tell him more about her. Several of the photos were pictures of Della with a trio of other women, all about her age. But it took him a few moments to realize one of the women in the pictures *was* Della, since she looked different than she did now—her hair was short and black, not the shoulder-length deep gold it was now. But why would she cover up a color like that? Or wear it so short?

Women.

Judging by the length of her hair now, the photos on her phone must be at least a year old. In a few of them, Della and the other women were dressed in business attire and seated at a table with girly-looking drinks sitting in front of them, appearing as if they were blowing off steam at the end of a workday. Okay, so Della had a job and wasn't necessarily the idle socialite he'd thought her to be. It didn't mean she hadn't come from money. She might have even been a client of some kind of one or more of the other women.

Scrolling further down through the pictures, Marcus finally found what he was looking for. Photos of Della, still with short, dark hair, seated with a man on a beach somewhere. A man who looked old enough to be her father, but who was good-looking and fit. Obviously very rich. Obviously very powerful. Obviously very married.

Marcus knew those things about the guy because he knew the guy's type. Too well. He worked and dealt with men like him every day. A lot of them were his friends. This had to be Geoffrey. Who else would it be? No one else in Della's contact list was identified informally by first name except for her girlfriends.

He navigated to her call list and saw that the last time Geoffrey had called Della was three nights ago. The last time Della had called him was yesterday morning. And the morning before that. And the morning before that. He kept scrolling. She'd called Geoffrey every single morning, weekday or weekend, always either at nine o'clock or within minutes before or after that hour.

Whoever Geoffrey was, he was keeping tabs on her. And he was making sure she was the one who called him, not the other way around. Another way to exert his control over her. Della hadn't made or received phone calls from anyone else for more than three months, at least, that was how far back her call log went. Whoever this guy was, he'd had her disconnected from her friends and family for a long time.

Was that why she had come to Chicago? To escape an abusive lover? But she'd told Marcus last night that one night was all she could give him, and she'd phoned Geoffrey yesterday, so obviously this guy wasn't out of her life yet.

He glanced at the clock on the nightstand. It was approaching 8:45 a.m. In fifteen minutes, Della would have to make her obligatory daily call. But it was a safe bet she wouldn't do it unless Marcus was out of the room—not if she didn't want him to overhear her. He'd been planning to take a shower after she was finished, but now he was thinking maybe he'd wait a bit. 'Til, say, well after nine o'clock. It would be interesting to see how Geoffrey—whoever the hell he was—would react to Della's lack of cooperation. Maybe he'd call her instead. And that, Marcus thought, was something he definitely wanted to be around for.

It wasn't so much that he wanted to confirm his suspicions that Della was attached to another man in some way—a thought that made the breakfast he'd consumed rebel on him. It was because if someone *was* mistreating her, whether emotionally or mentally or physically, Marcus wanted to know about it. Then he wanted to know the guy's full name. And address. So he could hop in his car the minute the roads were clear, and beat the holy hell out of the guy.

When the shower cut off, Marcus hastily closed the phone and returned it to Della's purse with her other belongings. Then he placed it on the dresser in exactly the same position it had been before. Quickly, he grabbed the newspaper that had been brought up with breakfast and returned to the bed, picked up his coffee and pretended to read.

By the time Della emerged from the shower wrapped in her blue robe again and scrubbing her damp hair with a towel, he'd managed to stow the rage he'd begun to feel for that son of a bitch Geoffrey—at least for the time being.

"The shower is all yours," she said as she drew nearer to the bed.

"Thanks," Marcus replied without looking up from the paper.

From the corner of his eye, he saw her glance at the clock. Mere minutes away from nine. He kept his gaze fixed blindly on the newspaper.

Della's agitation at his tepid response was an almost palpable thing. "You, ah, you might want to hurry. You wouldn't want them to run out of hot water." He looked up long enough to see her shift her weight nervously from one foot to the other. "Since it looks like no one will be checking out today. There are probably quite a few people using the shower."

He turned his attention back to the paper. "I don't think a hotel like the Ambassador got to be a hotel like the Ambassador by running out of hot water on its guests. It'll be fine."

"But still…"

"First I want to finish this article about—" Just what was he pretending to read, anyway? Damn. He'd picked up the Style section. "This article about the return of the, uh, the chunky metallic necklace," he said, somehow without losing a drop of testosterone. "Wow, did those ever go out of style in the first place? And then," he continued, "there were a couple of pieces in the Business section that looked even more interesting." He looked at Della again and saw that panicked look from last night creeping into her expression. "It's not like I have anywhere to go," he said. "And it's been a while since I've been able to take my time with the Sunday *Tribune*."

"But…" Her voice trailed off without her finishing. "Okay. Then I'll, ah, I'll dry my hair." She pointed halfheartedly over her shoulder. "I have a hairbrush in my purse."

Marcus nodded, pretending to be absorbed by the fashion icon that was the chunky metallic necklace.

The moment her back was turned, though, he looked up in time to see her withdraw both her brush and phone from the purse, then stash the cell in her robe pocket. When she started to spin around again, he quickly moved his gaze to the paper.

"You know what?" she said suddenly. "I love ice in my orange juice, so I'm going to run down the hall and see if there's an ice machine on this floor."

And then, Marcus thought, she would duck into a stairwell to check in with the man who was trying to control her life.

"Call room service to bring some up," he told her, still looking at the paper.

"I don't want to trouble them with something like that. They must be busy getting everyone's breakfast to them."

Now Marcus put down the paper. "Then I'll get some ice for you."

"No," she said, a little too quickly and a little too adamantly. She seemed to realize she'd over-reacted, because she forced a smile and said,

"I'm, ah, I'm starting to feel a bit of cabin fever. A little walk down the hall will be nice."

"In your robe and bare feet?" he asked, dipping his head toward her attire—or lack thereof.

"No one will see," she said as she began to sidestep toward the door. "Everyone else is probably sleeping in."

"Not if they're keeping room service hopping and using up all the hot water the way you say."

"You know what I mean."

"We're not sleeping in," he pointed out.

"Yes, but we—" She stopped abruptly, obviously not wanting to bring up the reason they'd woken early. Or maybe it was just that she wasn't any more certain about what the two of them were doing than Marcus was. "I mean…even if someone does see me," she said, trying a different tack, "what difference does it make? It's a hotel. It's Sunday morning. There must be plenty of people still in their robes and bare feet."

Not when there was a blizzard raging outside, Marcus wanted to say. The only reason he and Della weren't dressed was because they didn't have anything to change into. But he didn't point out any of those things. If he kept trying to prevent her from leaving the room, she would come up with more reasons why she needed to get out. And if he pressed her, she was only going to get suspicious of him.

"Fine," he said, looking at the paper again… and seeing nothing but red. "Don't forget to take the key."

"Of course," she said as she collected that from the dresser, too. "I won't be but a minute."

If she was able to make that promise, Marcus thought, then her conversations with Geoffrey must not involve much. Just enough for the guy to make sure she did what she was told.

He waited only until the door clicked shut behind her, then hurried over to silently open it, enough that he could see her making her way down the hall. She'd already withdrawn the phone from her pocket and was dialing one-handed, meaning she'd still be in sight when her conversation began, so Marcus was bound to miss some of it. Impatiently, he waited until she rounded a corner at the end of the hall, then he slipped the metal rod of the chain lock between it and the jamb and stole after her at twice her pace.

When he peered around the corner, he saw her duck through another door that led to the stairwell and heard her speaking into the phone. But she was speaking softly enough that he couldn't distinguish a word. So he raced after her and halted by the door through which she'd exited and cocked his head close. Unfortunately, he could still only hear incomprehensible murmuring. So, as quietly as he could, he turned the knob and pushed the door open a crack, to see that she had seated herself on the top step with her back to him. So he opened it a little bit more.

"Really, Geoffrey, I'm fine," he heard her say. "There's no reason for you to come over. You'd get stuck in the snow if you tried."

He tried to discern something in her voice that sounded fearful or cowering, but, really, she did sound fine.

"I mean, yeah, the snow is kind of a drag," she continued, "but it's not like you ever let me go anywhere anyway."

So she wasn't supposed to be out and about, Marcus thought. His suspicions were confirmed.

"I had groceries delivered this week," she said, "and I downloaded a couple of books. Thanks for the Kindle and the Netflix subscription, by the way. It's helped a lot."

It was the least the son of a bitch could do, since he wouldn't let her go anywhere.

"What?" he heard Della ask. Then she laughed lightly. "No, nothing like that. That's the last thing I need. Mostly romantic comedies. I need something light and escapist, all things considered."

She paused, though whether it was because Geoffrey was talking or because she was looking for something else to say, Marcus didn't know. Finally, though, she began to speak again. "Okay, if you must know, *Bridget Jones's Diary, Love, Actually* and *Pride and Prejudice.*" There was another pause, then she laughed again. "Yes. I love Colin Firth. So does your wife, if you'll recall."

It really wasn't the kind of conversation Marcus had expected to hear her having with a married man who was keeping her a virtual prisoner. But neither did it quite dispel his suspicions that Della was being controlled. What really bothered him, though, was that there was something different in her voice when she spoke to Geoffrey that wasn't there when she was talking to him. A casualness and easiness, a lack of formality, that she hadn't exhibited with Marcus. As if she were actually more comfortable with the other man than she was with him. As if she and Geoffrey shared a relationship that was based less on control and more on trust.

Just what the hell was this guy to her?

Then Marcus heard her say something that chilled him.

"Look, Geoffrey, how much longer am I going to have to live this way? You told me I'd only have to do this for six months. That was eleven months ago. You promised me that if I did everything you guys told me to—"

Guys? So Geoffrey wasn't the only one? She was being passed around among a group? Had he really heard that right?

"—that then I'd be free," she continued. "But I'm still—"

The other man must have cut her off before she could finish, because Della stopped talking and listened obediently without saying a word for several minutes. He saw her lift a hand to her head and push back her hair with a jerky motion that suggested she was anxious. She murmured a few uh-huhs, then slumped forward with her free hand braced on her knee and her forehead pressed to her palm.

Finally, with clear dejection—and maybe a little fear?—she replied, "Two weeks? That's all the time I have left?"

Until what? Marcus wanted to yell. What the hell was she talking about? What the hell did the man expect her to do that made her sound so unwilling to do it?

"Then it's really going to happen," she said with clear resignation, sounding more reserved than ever. "I'm really going to have to do it."

Do what, for God's sake?

"No, I understand," she said. "I'll go through with it. I mean, it's not like I have much choice, do I?" There was another pause, then she continued, "I know I promised. And I'll hold up my end of the bargain. I just...I didn't think it would be like this, Geoffrey. I didn't think I'd feel like this about everything." More softly, she added, "I didn't think I'd feel like this about myself." Then, because Geoffrey must not have heard that last, she said with unmistakable melancholy. "It was nothing important. Never mind."

Nothing important. Marcus felt a little sick to his stomach. The way she felt about herself wasn't important. This guy had her so wound around his finger that Della didn't even realize how unbalanced and unhealthy the relationship was.

Relationship, hell. What she had with this guy was a bargain. She'd said so herself. And it was obviously a bad one. A least on her end.

"So two weeks then," she said again. "I have two weeks to get myself ready and in the right frame of mind."

Marcus hated to think what that getting ready would involve. He hated more to think about what the *right frame of mind* for such a thing would be.

He heard her answer a few more yes-and-no questions—with little more than a yes or no, sounding more and more like a child with each one—then heard her promise she would call tomorrow morning at the usual time. Then he heard the sound of her phone flipping closed.

He was about to pull the door to and hurry to the room before she caught him eavesdropping, but he heard something else that stopped him short—the very soft sound of muffled crying.

Something twisted inside him. He wasn't accustomed to hearing a woman cry. Mostly because he made sure he got involved with women who were as shallow as he was. At least where things like emotional involvement were concerned. Obviously, Della wasn't shallow. Obviously, she cared a lot about things like involvement. Even if she was currently involved with the wrong man.

Putting aside, for now, the fact that that word probably applied to himself as much as it did Geoffrey, Marcus pushed open the door and silently moved through it. He didn't know why. It would have been best for him and Della both if he went back to the room and pretended he knew nothing of her conversation. It would have been best if they spent the rest of the weekend pretending there was nothing beyond that room until the two of them had to leave it.

But when he saw her sitting on the stair landing with her feet propped on the carpeted step below her, her arms crossed over her knees, her head rested on her arms, her shoulders shaking lightly, he knew he could never go back to pretending anything. She still had the cell phone clasped in one hand, but it fell, landing with a dull thud when she began to cry harder, and she didn't bother to retrieve it. Instead, she surrendered to her sobs, muffling them by pressing her mouth to the sleeve of her robe. She was so lost in her despair that she had no idea Marcus stood behind her.

He didn't know what to do or say, could only stand there feeling helpless. It was an alien concept, this helplessness, and he didn't like it at all. His instincts told him to flee before she saw him, but his conscience—and he was surprised to discover he actually had one—dictated he do something to make her feel better. He let the two war with each other, to see who would win, but when instinct and conscience kept bickering, he stepped in and made the decision himself. He took a tentative step forward, then another.

As he was reaching down to curl his fingers over her shoulder, she whirled her head quickly around. When she saw him there, her eyes went wide with panic, and she stood so quickly, she almost pitched backward down the stairs. He wrapped his fingers around her wrist as she managed to right herself, but neither seemed to know what to say or do after that. For a long moment, they only stood silently looking at each other. Then, finally, Della stepped onto the landing with Marcus. He released her wrist, but brushed away a tear from her cheek with the pad of his thumb.

He had no idea what to say. He, Marcus Fallon, who had never been at a loss for words in his life. The man who could find a quip—whether appropriate or not—to alleviate any tense situation, who could make light of even the most difficult circumstances, couldn't scrape up one word that would ease the tension in this one. Some knight in shining armor he was turning out to be. But then, he'd never wanted to be a knight in shining armor.

Not until now.

"Are you okay?" he asked softly, threading his fingers into her damp hair.

Her eyes were huge, seeming larger thanks to the presence of her tears, making her look vulnerable and fragile. He knew she was neither of those things, and realizing that one conversation with Geoffrey could make her feel that way made him despise the man even more.

She nodded, but said nothing, only swiped at her wet eyes with both hands before shoving them into the pockets of her robe.

"You don't look okay," Marcus said. He lifted his other hand and wove those fingers through her hair, too, until he found the nape of her neck and cradled it in his palm.

"I'm fine," she assured him quietly, sounding anything but.

Knowing it would be pointless to pretend he hadn't heard her on the phone, he asked, "Who were you talking to?"

She looked at the phone on the floor, then up at Marcus. "How much of that did you hear?"

He thought about telling her he'd heard enough to know she was mixed up with someone she shouldn't be who was obliging her to do something she obviously didn't want to do, but that was kind of like the pot calling the kettle black. She shouldn't be mixed up with Marcus, either. Not being the kind of woman she was. Namely, the kind whose emotions ran deeper than a sheaf of paper.

"Not very much," he lied. "I got worried when you didn't come back, so I came looking for you."

"Was I gone that long?"

He smiled, unable to help himself. "A few seconds was too long to be away from you."

When she didn't smile back, his own fell. "So who were you talking to, Della?"

"No one," she said. "No one important."

"He's the one you were worried about missing you today, isn't he?"

She hesitated for a moment, then nodded. "But not the way—" She expelled an irritated sound.

"Not the way what?" Marcus asked.

"Nothing." She pulled away from him, then bent down to scoop up her phone and the still-empty ice bucket. She looked at his face, but her gaze immediately ricocheted to the door. "Look, Marcus, can we go back to the room and forget this happened?"

When he said nothing, she looked at him again, her eyebrows arrowed downward. "Can we? Please?"

He crossed his arms over his chest, telling himself the gesture was *not* defensive. Marcus Fallon didn't get defensive. Marcus Fallon was the most offensive human being on the planet. "I don't know, Della. Can we?"

She glanced away again. "I can if you can."

Somehow, he doubted that. Because in addition to being the man who currently claimed Della as his own, Geoffrey seemed like the kind of man who wouldn't let her forget about anything.

In spite of that, Marcus nodded. Once. "Fine. Let's just forget it happened."

Still not looking at him, she replied, "You promise?"

"I do."

When she looked at him again, all traces of her former sadness were gone. She looked matter-of-fact and a little blank. She sounded that way, too, when she said, "Thank you. I appreciate it."

It was only then, when she sounded so formal, that Marcus realized she had, for a few moments, been as familiar with him as she had been with the man on the phone. But now the reserve was in her voice again. When he looked at her, he realized it was in her posture, too. They were indeed back to pretending. He should be relieved about that.

Instead, for some reason, now Marcus kind of wanted to cry.

Six

The mood in the room was considerably darker when they returned, Della couldn't help noticing. As was the room itself. She strode directly to the window and pulled back the curtains to find her worst fears confirmed. She wouldn't have thought it possible, but the snow was coming down even thicker and faster now than it had been when she'd first awoken.

She was never going to get out of here.

But then, what did she care? It wasn't as though she had anything waiting for her out there. Nothing but a nondescript house full of nondescript furnishings in a nondescript Chicago suburb populated by nondescript families. Middle-class, middle-income, middle America. The area had been chosen specifically because it was so unremarkable and unmemorable. Della had been living there for eleven months now, and even she would have been hard-pressed to describe from memory what any of her neighbors or their houses looked like. It was the last place she wanted to be, the last place she should be living, the last place anyone would think to look for her.

That, of course, was the whole point.

What made it worse was that she'd been expressly forbidden to interact with anyone or set foot outside unless absolutely unavoidable, and never without asking Geoffrey for permission first. So far, he hadn't considered a single one of her reasons to be absolutely unavoidable. Hence the sneaking around on those occasions when staying in the house would have driven her unavoidably insane.

As disconcerting as it was to be stuck here with Marcus until tomorrow—at least—a part of her thrilled at the prospect. She'd never felt as free or unencumbered—or uninhibited—as she did with him. She scarcely recognized herself this morning. Never in her life had she behaved with a man the way she had behaved with him. Not only the part about having sex with someone she'd just met, but also the sheer volume of sex they'd had. And the earthiness of it. The carnality of it. She'd *never* done things with other men that she'd done with Marcus last night. But with him, she'd felt no reticence or self-consciousness at all. Probably because he hadn't had any himself. On the contrary—he'd been demanding and exacting when it came to what he wanted. But he'd been every bit as generous when giving himself to her.

Something warm and fizzy bubbled inside, an unfamiliar percolation of both desire and contentment, of want and satisfaction. She'd felt it on and off throughout the night, usually between bouts of lovemaking when their bodies had been damp and entwined. But Marcus was on the other side of the room now, and their exchange in the stairwell had been a less than satisfying one. Even so, she could still feel this way, simply by being in the same room with him, knowing he wasn't leaving her. Not yet.

So really, why was she so eager to leave?

Maybe, she answered herself, it was because a part of her still knew this couldn't last forever and saw no point in prolonging it. The longer it went on, the harder it would be when it came time for the two of them to part. And they would have to part. Soon. The fantasy she and Marcus had carved out last night should have been over already. They should have separated before dawn, before the harsh light of day cast shadows over what they had created together.

They both had obligations that didn't involve the other—Della to Geoffrey and Marcus to the faceless woman for whom he obviously still had deep feelings. Even if he was no longer "with" her, as he claimed, it was clear he still cared very much for her. Too much for the possibility of including someone new in his life. Even if Della was in a position to become that someone new, which she definitely was not. Not here. Not now. Not ever.

How much *had* he heard of her conversation

with Geoffrey? she wondered as she turned from the window and saw Marcus pouring himself another cup of coffee. She tried to remember if she'd said anything that might have offered a hint of what her life had become, but she was confident he would never suspect the truth. Because the truth was like something straight out of fiction.

He glanced up suddenly, and when he saw her looking at him, lifted the coffee carafe and asked, "Would you like some?"

It was a mundane question from a man who looked as if this was just another typical morning in his life. But Della could practically feel a vibe emanating from him that reached all the way across the room, and it was neither mundane nor typical. It was cool and distant, and it was, she was certain, a remnant of their exchange in the stairwell.

Was this how it would be for the rest of their time together? Strained and difficult? Please, no, she immediately answered herself. Somehow, they had to recapture their earlier magic. If only for a little while.

"Yes," she said, even though her stomach was roiling too much for her to consume anything. She only wanted some kind of conversation with him that wasn't anxious. "Please."

She strode to the breakfast cart, standing as close to Marcus as she dared, watching him pour. He had magnificent hands, strong with sturdy fingers and no adornments. Looking at his hands, she would never have guessed he worked for a brokerage house. He had the hands of someone who used them for something other than pushing the keys of a computer or cell phone all day.

"Do you play any sports?" she asked impulsively.

His expression was surprised as he handed her her coffee. "I thought you didn't want to know anything about me."

Oh, yeah. She didn't. She already knew more than she wanted to. So maybe it wouldn't hurt to know a little bit more. Ignoring the convoluted logic in that, she said, "I changed my mind."

He handed her her coffee with a resigned sigh. "Squash," he told her. "Three times a week. With another one of the—" He halted, as if he'd been about to reveal something else about himself, but this time it was something he *didn't* want her to know. "With a coworker," he finally finished. He sipped his coffee, then met her gaze levelly. "Why do you ask?"

"Your hands," she said before she could stop herself. "You have good hands, Marcus. They're not the hands of an office worker."

His eyes seemed to go a little darker at that, and she remembered that there were other ways his hands were good, too. Lots and lots of other ways. She spun around, striding away on slightly shaky legs. But when she realized she was walking straight toward the bed, she quickly sidetracked toward two chairs arranged on each side of a table near the window.

"It's still snowing," she said as she sat. "Maybe even harder than before."

Marcus strode to the window, lifted one curtain for a scant moment, then let it drop. "I guess we could turn on the TV to see what the weather guys are saying about how much longer this will last."

"I suppose we could."

But neither of them did. They only looked at each other expectantly, almost as if they were daring the other to do it. Della knew why she didn't. She wondered if Marcus's reason mirrored her own.

Finally, he folded himself into the other chair, setting his cup on the table beside hers. He crossed his legs with deceptive casualness, propped an elbow on the chair arm to rest his chin in his hand and, looking her right in the eye, asked, "Who's Geoffrey?"

Della felt as if someone punched her right in the stomach. Obviously he'd heard more of the phone conversation than he'd let on. She wondered how much. She wondered even harder about how she was supposed to explain her relationship with Geoffrey to Marcus. It wasn't as though she could be vague about something like that.

She reminded herself she didn't have to tell Marcus anything. Not the truth, not a fabrication, nothing. She could say it was none of his business, repeat their agreement not to disclose any personal details about each other—which he'd already breached a number of times, one of which had been at her own encouragement—and change the subject.

But she was surprised to discover there was a part of herself that wanted to tell him about Geoffrey. And not just Geoffrey, but about everything that had led to her meeting him. She wanted to tell Marcus everything about the mess that had started on New Year's Day to herald the beginning of the worst year of her life, about the months of fear and uncertainty that had followed, right up until her encounter with him at Palumbo's. She wanted to tell him about how she hadn't felt safe or contented for eleven months. About how lonely she'd been. About how hopeless and scared she'd felt.

At least until her encounter with him at Palumbo's. It was only now that Della realized she hadn't experienced any of those feelings since meeting Marcus. For the first time in eleven months—maybe for the first time in her life—she'd been free of anxiety and pleasantly at ease. She'd spent the past twelve hours ensconced in a perfect bubble of completeness, where nothing intruded that could cause her harm or pain. All because of a man whose last name she didn't even know.

But she couldn't tell him any of that, either.

She couldn't say a word. She'd taken a virtual vow of silence about what had happened in New York, and she'd been told that if she revealed anything to anyone, it could compromise every-thing. And then the last eleven months of living in hiding and being so relentlessly alone would have been for nothing.

Two weeks, she reminded herself. That was how long Geoffrey had told her she had to wait. Only two more weeks. In sixteen days, every-thing would be revealed, everything would come to light, and Della would be free of all of them. Of Geoffrey, of Egan Collingwood, of her boss Mr. Nathanson and everyone else at Whitworth and Stone. And even if that freedom meant losing everything she had now and starting all over somewhere else, even if it meant becom-ing an entirely new person, at least she would be done with all of it. She would be safe. She would be free. She would be *done.* She just had to hold on for two more weeks.

She opened her mouth to tell Marcus that Geoffrey was none of his business and then change the subject, but instead she hedged, "Well. So much for forgetting about the episode in the stairwell. And you promised."

"I've made a lot of promises since meeting you," he reminded her. "And I haven't kept many of them. You should probably know that about me. I'm great at making promises. Terrible at keeping them."

She nodded. "Good to know."

"Doesn't make me a terrible person," he told her. "It just makes me more human."

It also made him an excellent reminder, Della thought. His assertion that he couldn't keep promises illustrated more clearly why she couldn't tell him anything more about herself. She might very well become the topic of his next cocktail party anecdote or an inadvertently shared story with a colleague who had some connection to the very life she was trying to escape. Not because he was a bad person, as he had said. But because he was human. And humanity was something Della had learned not to trust.

"So who is he, Della?"

She hesitated, trying to remind herself again of all the reasons why she couldn't tell Marcus the truth—or anything else. Then, very softly, she heard herself say, "Geoffrey is a man who… who kind of…" She sighed again. "He kind of takes care of me."

Marcus said nothing for a moment, then nodded slowly. His expression cleared some, and he looked as if he completely understood. That was impossible, because there was still a lot of it that even Della didn't understand.

"You're his mistress, you mean," Marcus said in a remarkably matter-of-fact way. "It's all right, Della. I'm a big boy. You can spell it out for me."

It took a moment for what he was saying to sink in. And not only because the word *mistress* was so old-fashioned, either. Marcus thought she and Geoffrey had a sexual relationship. That he was a wealthy benefactor who was giving her money and gifts in exchange for sexual favors.

That she, Della Hannan, the only girl in her neighborhood who had been determined to claw her way out of the slum *not* using sex as the means to get there, was now making her way in the world by renting herself out sexually to the highest bidder.

She should have been insulted. Instead, she wanted to laugh. Because compared to the reality of her situation, his assumption, as tawdry as it sounded, was just so…so… So adorably innocent.

Wow. If she *were* Geoffrey's mistress, that would make her life a million times easier. But number one, the guy was married. Number two, he was old enough to be her father. Number three, he looked like a sixty-something version of Dwight Schrute. And number four, there was no way he could afford a mistress when he had two kids in college and a daughter getting married in six months. After all, federal marshals weren't exactly the highest paid people on the government payroll.

Marcus must have mistaken her lack of response as being offended instead of off guard, because he hastily continued, "Look, Della, it doesn't matter to me. I'm the last person who should, or would, judge the way another person lives their life. I don't consider your situation to be appalling or bad or cheap or dirty or embarrassing or—" He seemed to realize how badly he was belaboring his objections—and he'd barely made a dent if he was going to be all alphabetical about it—something that made them sound even less convincing than they already did. He gave his head a single shake, as if he were trying to clear it. "Besides, it's not like I haven't, ah, kept a woman myself in the past."

Della wasn't sure, but he almost sounded as if he were about to offer her such a job now.

He tried again, holding out one hand as if he were literally groping for the right words. "What I'm trying to say is that I don't think any less of you for it. Sometimes, in order to survive in this world, people have to resort to unconventional methods. It doesn't make them any less a human being than anyone else. In a lot of ways, it makes them better than the people who don't have to struggle to make their way. Because they're…

they're survivors, Della. That's what they do. They…they survive. That's what you are, too. You're a survivor. You're unconventional and you're…you're making your way in the world, and you're… You're surviving. You're—"

"No man's mistress," she finished for him, interrupting him before he broke into song. Or broke a blood vessel in his brain trying to cope. Whatever. "That's not how Geoffrey takes care of me, Marcus. We don't have a sexual relationship *at all*. I mean, Geoffrey is his last name. I don't even call him by his first name." It was Winston, and probably why he asked everyone to call him by his last name.

Marcus's relief was almost palpable. So much for not thinking less of anyone who survived in the world through unconventional methods. She might have laughed if he hadn't been right about one thing: She was surviving. And she did depend on Geoffrey's presence in her life to accomplish that.

Della couldn't give Marcus any details about what had happened in New York or the fact that she was a material witness in a federal case that involved her former Wall Street employer, Whitworth and Stone, and her former boss, Donald Nathanson. Especially knowing as she did now that Marcus worked for the equally illustrious Fallon Brothers. It wasn't unlikely that he knew people at Whitworth and Stone and moved in the same circles. Not that she feared he would report her to anyone, since no one there even knew—yet—about the case the feds were building. As far as anyone at Whitworth and Stone was concerned, the reason Della had stopped showing up for work without giving notice was because of personal reasons that would make performing her job intolerable. After all, Egan had been one of Whitworth and Stone's up-and-coming executives.

She had no way of knowing how Marcus would react to the revelation that Della had, in her position as executive assistant to one of the company's vice presidents, discovered a trail of illegal money laundering for unsavory overseas groups and the gross misuse of government bailout funds. She couldn't tell him about how she'd smuggled out files over a period of two weeks,

or about going to the FBI with what she'd uncovered, or about how they'd immediately put
her into protective custody with the U.S. Marshals and moved her out of New York to keep
her under wraps until she could appear before
the grand jury. She couldn't tell him how she'd
been in hiding for the past eleven months while
the feds built their case.

And she for sure couldn't tell him about how,
once the trial was over—and Geoffrey had just
told her the grand jury was convening in two
weeks—she was probably going to be placed in
the Witness Security Program, for safe measure.
Even though her life hadn't been threatened, and
even though none of the crimes committed had
been violent ones, being a whistle-blower wasn't
exactly the most celebrated gig in the world.
There was no way she'd ever find work in the
financial world again.

And, well, even though it was unlikely, there
was no guarantee there wouldn't be some
other kind of retaliation against her. Some of
the groups to which Whitworth and Stone had
diverted funds had done some pretty terrible

things in other parts of the world. It would be best for her to start over somewhere as a new person, with a new identity and a new life. A place where nobody knew her real name and where there was no chance she would ever be discovered.

A place completely removed from the spotlight Marcus so joyfully embraced in his own life. The last thing Della could afford was to have someone see her with him and recognize her from her former position. It would be even worse for her to be recognized after she'd given her testimony and put a lot of powerful people behind bars. At best, she would be a social pariah. At worst… Well, she didn't want to think about things like that.

Bottom line, there was no way this thing with Marcus could last beyond a weekend. He would never give up the big, showy lifestyle he loved. And she was a woman who had to avoid a big, showy life at all costs.

"Well, if Geoffrey isn't your…benefactor," Marcus said now, "then who is he? A relative?"

Stalling, she asked, "Why do you want to

know? What difference does it make? Once the snow lets up, you and I are never going to—"

"I just want to know, Della."

"But why?"

"Maybe because you burst into tears after talking to the guy?"

Oh, right. That. That had kind of startled Della, too. But for some reason, during this morning's talk with Geoffrey, she had begun to feel keenly how truly alone she was. Geoffrey had been her only tie to the outside world for eleven months— at least until she met Marcus—and the conversations she had with him never lasted any longer than it took for her to check in every day and let him know she was okay. She always wanted to talk longer, since she never got to talk to anyone. Just to hear a human voice that wasn't coming from an electronic device. Every time, Geoffrey cut short the conversation because there was no reason to prolong it. Especially on weekends, he wanted to be with his family. Geoffrey always had things to do, places to go, people to see after he hung up. And Della always had to go back to the vast nothingness of waiting, all alone.

But this morning, after hanging up, she'd realized she *didn't* have to go back to being alone. This morning, she'd known Marcus was waiting for her. Someone who would talk to her. Someone who would share breakfast with her. Someone who would care for her. Be with her. Touch her. If only for a little while. And the thought that she would have such intimacy—even if it was only temporary and superficial—only made it worse to think about leaving it, leaving him, behind. Something about that was so intolerable. So bleak. So heartbreaking. Della simply hadn't been able to stop the tears from coming.

She felt the sting of tears threatening again and shoved the thought to the furthest, darkest corner of her brain. "He's not a relative, either," she said wearily.

When she didn't elaborate, Marcus asked, "Then how and why is he taking care of you?"

She expelled an impatient sound. "I don't guess you'd settle for 'It's complicated,' would you?"

He shook his head. "The directions for assembling a nuclear warhead are complicated," he told her. "Life? Not so much."

She managed a smile. "Trust me, Marcus. My life is currently *very* complicated."

"In what way?"

She couldn't tell him. She couldn't even hint. Maybe if he didn't have the job he had. Maybe if he wasn't a rich guy who didn't keep his finger on the pulse of the financial world. Maybe if he was just some average guy with an average job who didn't for a minute understand the workings of Wall Street…

She still couldn't tell him, she knew. So she stalled. "The place where I come from on the East Coast I had to leave a while back, because I—I got into some trouble there."

His expression wavered not at all. "You did something illegal?"

"No," she was quick to assure him. "Nothing like that. But I—I got caught up in something… not good…without intending to. So Geoffrey found me a place to live until things blow over. And I call him every day so he knows I'm okay."

"That doesn't sound complicated," Marcus said. "That sounds dangerous."

Della opened her mouth to contradict him,

then realized she couldn't do that without lying. The chances of her being in danger were very small. The main reason the feds wanted to keep her under wraps was so no one at Whitworth and Stone would catch on to the fact that they were being investigated. And, too, to make sure Della didn't skip out on them after promising to give testimony.

"Not dangerous," she said. "They just want to be sure."

"And by *they,* you would mean…who?" Marcus asked. "The police?"

She shook her head, but didn't elaborate. It wasn't the police keeping an eye on her. Not technically. She was much further up the law enforcement ladder than that.

"Then who?"

"I can't tell you any more than that," she said. "I only said that much because I wanted you to know the truth about Geoffrey. I'm not…tied to him. Not that way."

Marcus hesitated a moment. "Are you…tied to anyone…that way?"

She should tell him yes. Make him think she

was involved with someone who meant a great deal to her. Maybe that would make it easier when the time came for them to part. If Marcus thought she was going home to another man, and if he thought she was shallow enough to have sex with him when she was involved with someone else, then it would be easier for him to put her in his past and keep her there.

If only she could do the same with him.

But instead of lying, her damnable honesty surfaced again. "There's no one," she said. "There hasn't been for a long time."

That, she supposed, was why she capitulated to Marcus so quickly and easily the night before. Because he was the first person she'd had face-to-face contact with for months. The first person who'd conversed with her. Who'd smiled at her. Who'd laughed with her. Who'd touched her. She'd gone too long without the most basic human need—the need to bond with someone else. Even if it was only over an article in a tabloid while waiting in line at the supermarket or sharing a few words while making change for another person at the Laundromat. People needed to be with other people in order to feel whole. Della hadn't had that for too long.

Marcus eyed her thoughtfully for another moment, then said, "So if it wasn't legal trouble, then what kind of trouble was it?"

"I can't tell you any more than I have, Marcus."

"Why not?"

"Because…it's complicated."

He dragged his chair around the table until it was directly facing hers, then sat close enough that their knees were touching. He took both of her hands in his.

"Look, there's a good chance I can help you out. I know a lot of people on the East Coast. Good friends. People I trust and who can pull strings. Some owe me favors. Others I know things about they'd rather not see made public so they'd be happy to grant me favors."

"I'm not sure those sound like friends to me."

"Maybe not. But I can still trust them to do what I tell them to. A lot of them are people with clout. They know people who know people who know people who can get things done."

And it was precisely that network of people

who knew other people that was what Della was afraid of. Marcus might inadvertently tip her hand to the very people who were under investigation. His friends might be their friends, too. They were people like him—rich, powerful, enjoying an elevated social standing they didn't want to have compromised. They worked in the same industry. They were of the same tribe. Hell, he might not even want to help her if he found out what was at stake.

"You can't help," she said. "I appreciate the offer, Marcus, but you can't."

"How do you know?"

"I just do."

He studied her for another moment. "It's because you don't trust me. Because you just met me and don't know anything about me. But that doesn't have to be the case, Della. I—"

"It isn't that." And she was surprised to realize that was the truth. She did trust Marcus. In spite of having just met him. And she knew more about him after one night than she did about a lot of people she'd known in New York for years. But money made people do funny things. Lots of money made people do bad things. And billions of dollars… That made people do desperate things.

"There must be something I can do, Della," he insisted, his voice laced with something akin to pleading. "The thought of you being in trouble somehow…it isn't right."

Unable to help herself, she leaned forward and cupped his strong jaw in her hand. "You're a good guy, Marcus. And it's nice of you, wanting to help. But this is on me. Eventually, things will be better, but for now…"

She didn't finish. Mostly because, for now, she wanted to forget. She had another day and night to spend with Marcus, here in this hotel room where nothing from the outside could get to them. For now, she only wanted to think about that.

He covered her hand with his, then turned his face to place a soft kiss at the center of her palm. Warmth ebbed through her at the gesture. It was so sweet. So tender. So unlike their couplings of the night before.

"There must be something I can do to help,"

he said again. "Please, Della. Just tell me what to do."

She reached out with her other hand and threaded it through his hair, letting the silky tresses sift through her fingers before moving them to his forehead, his jaw, his mouth. "You can make love to me, again," she said softly. "You can hold me and touch me and say meaningless things that both of us know aren't true anywhere but here in this room. You can make me feel safe and warm and cherished. You can make me forget that there's anything in the world except the two of us. Do that for me and I'll—"

She stopped herself before saying *I'll love you forever.* Even though she was confident he would know it was hyperbole, it didn't feel like something she should put out there in the world.

He smiled, but there was something in the gesture that was a little hollow. His eyes were dark with wanting, however, when he reached for her and murmured, "Well, if you insist…"

Seven

Without hesitation, Marcus leaned forward and covered Della's mouth with his, dipping his hands into the deep V of her robe to curl his fingers over her bare shoulders as he deepened the kiss. Her skin was warm and fragrant from her recent shower, and the soft scent grew both stronger and more delicate as he slowly spread open the fabric of the garment. He traced the delicate line of her collarbone to the divot at the base of her throat, then his fingers stole around to her nape, spreading into the silk of her hair. It was still damp, and tangled around his fingers as if trying to trap his hand there forever. He wished they could stay embraced this way forever. He would never grow tired of touching her.

Della seemed to sense his thoughts, because her hands fell to the knot in her robe and untied it before she cupped his face in her palms. Spurred by her silent invitation, Marcus moved his hand lower, skimming the backs of his knuckles over the sensitive skin above her breasts before dragging his middle finger down the delicate valley between them. She gasped as he curved his fingers under one heavy breast and lifted it, then opened her mouth wider to invite him deep inside.

His last coherent thought was that he was responding to her the same way he had the night before, losing himself to her with a velocity and intensity that surpassed every other reaction, every other emotion, he had. The moment he touched her, everything else in the world ceased to exist. There was only heat and hunger, demand and desire, all of it commanding satisfaction.

Della seemed to understand that, too—or maybe she was feeling the same thing herself—because she was suddenly working feverishly at the sash of his robe, jerking it free so that she could dip her hands inside and explore him. Her fingers fumbled a bit as he gently began to knead her breast, but she recovered quickly, pushing his robe backward, over his shoulders and arms, spreading the fabric wider still. The next thing Marcus knew, she was on her knees in front of him, one hand curving over his taut thigh, the other moving on his hard shaft.

He nearly exploded at the contact, closing his eyes and sucking in a desperate breath as she gently palmed him. For long moments, she pleasured him that way, making his heart pound and his blood race until the rhythm of his passion roared in his ears. And when he felt her mouth close over him…

Oh, Della… Oh, baby…

When his fingers convulsed in her hair, she must have sensed how close he was to coming apart, because she stood and she took his hand in hers, then led him to the bed. When she pushed his robe completely from his shoulders and nudged him down to the mattress, he went willingly, watching with great interest as she shrugged out of her robe, too. She joined him in bed, but when she tried to face him, he cupped his hands over her shoulders, gently turned her around and positioned her on her hands and knees. Then he moved his hands to her hips and knelt behind her. He splayed his palms open on her back, skimming them up and down as he slowly entered her, then leaned forward until his chest was flush with her back. He caught her breasts in his hands and held them for a moment, thumbing her stiff nipples and eliciting a wild little sound from deep inside her. Then he withdrew himself slowly and thrust forward again. Hard.

She cried out at the depth of his penetration, curling her fingers into the fabric of the sheet. Marcus filled her again, even harder this time, eliciting a response from her that was hot, erotic and demanding. So what could Marcus do but obey her? He had never been with a woman who was so uninhibited about sex. Della both commanded and surrendered in ways no other woman ever had. She rode astride him, wrapped her legs around his waist when she was beneath him, demanded he take her kneeling and sitting and standing. When they finally surrendered to the climaxes that shook them simultaneously, she was bent over the chair where they had started as Marcus pummeled her from behind again. They came together, cried out their satisfaction together, rode out the waves of their orgasms together. Then, together, they relaxed and reined themselves in, and collapsed into the chair.

For long moments, they sat entwined, Marcus on the chair and Della in his lap, neither willing—or perhaps able—to say a word. Della opened her hand over the center of Marcus's chest, and he mimicked the gesture with her, noting how the rapid-fire beating of her heart kept time with his own. Gradually, it slowed along with his, too, until both of them were thumping along in happy, contented rhythm. At least, for now. Marcus suspected it wouldn't be long before their desires overtook them again.

But there had been something different in this coupling that hadn't been there before. He wasn't sure what it was or how it mattered, but it was there all the same. Yes, the sex had been hot, intense and carnal. Yes, they had both been consumed by an almost uncontrollable passion. Yes, they had said and done things they might not have said and done with other partners.

But there had been something else there that Marcus hadn't had with other partners, too. Not just a lack of inhibition, but a lack of fear. As if coming together with Della was simply a natural reaction to feelings he'd had for a very long time. He didn't know any other way to describe it, even though they'd known each other only a matter of hours. Sex with Della felt…right somehow. As if everything up until now had merely been a warm-up. *Della* felt right somehow. As if every woman before her had been practice. It meant something, he was sure of it. If he could only figure out what…

Marcus knew the moment he awoke that Della was gone. Even though it was still dark in the hotel room. Even though her fragrance still lingered on the pillow beside his own. Even though the sheets were still warm where she had lain. Maybe it had been the snick of the hotel room door closing behind her that woke him, he thought with surprising clarity for having just woken. Maybe if he hurried, he could still catch her before she made it to the elevator. Or if she had already disappeared into it, maybe he could hurry faster and catch her in the lobby before she made it out of the building.

But even as the thoughts raced through his head, he knew, too, that none of them were true. Because, somehow, he knew what had woken him wasn't a sound at all. What had woken him was the simple awareness, on some subconscious level, that Della was irretrievably gone and that he was irrevocably alone.

Alone, he marveled as he jackknifed up in the bed and palmed his eyes. It was a familiar condition, but it had never felt quite like this. It had never bothered Marcus to live alone or eat alone or work alone or do anything else alone. On the contrary, he'd always preferred his own company to that of others. Well, except for Charlotte, but that was because she had been a solitary creature herself. Marcus had never really felt as if he had that much in common with others, anyway. If he wanted companionship, it was easy to find it. There was always someone he could call or someplace he could go where, in a matter of minutes, he would be surrounded. Sometimes by friends, more often by acquaintances he pretended were friends, but the point was, he liked being alone.

He didn't like it this morning. Della's absence surrounded him like a rank, fetid carcass.

He rose and shrugged on his robe, knotting it around his waist as he moved to the window. In the sliver of moonlight that spilled through a slit in the curtains, he glimpsed a piece of paper lying on the table between the two chairs where he and Della had sat only hours ago. Something hitched tight in his chest as he reached for it, because he thought it was a note from her. But it was the paper on which he'd written his numbers for her the day before. She'd left it behind. Because she'd wanted to make clear to him that she wouldn't be contacting him in the future.

She'd said she'd found trouble in New York. He couldn't imagine what kind of trouble a woman like her could be in. But if Della said she was in trouble, then she was in trouble. And if she'd said he couldn't help her…

Well, there she could be wrong.

Marcus crumpled the paper in his palm and tossed it onto the table, then pulled back the drape. The sky was black and crystal clear beyond, dotted with stars that winked like gemstones under theater lights. Uncaring of the bitter cold, he unlatched the window and shoved it open as far as it would go—which was barely wide enough for him to stick his head through—then gazed down onto Michigan Avenue. He'd never seen the street deserted before, regardless of the hour, but it was now, even though the snowplows had been through. People had yet to brave their way out into the remnants of the blizzard and probably wouldn't until after the sun rose.

For some reason, Marcus looked to his right and saw the red lights of a retreating car disappear around a corner some blocks up. Another light atop it indicated it was a taxi. Della's taxi. He knew that as well as he knew his own name.

As well as he knew her name, too.

Never had he been more grateful for his lack of decorum than he was in that moment. Had he not rifled through her purse, he would have nothing of her now save her first name. Well, that and the memory of the most unforgettable weekend he'd ever spent with anyone. Now there was another reason he wouldn't forget it. Because he knew where to find Della Hannan. Maybe not in Chicago, but he did in New York. And that alone was worth its weight in gold. Provided one knew the right people.

And Marcus definitely knew the right people.

His cheeks began to burn in the freezing temperature, so he closed the window and retreated into the room. He scooped up his jacket from the back of the chair as he passed it, then sat on the side of the bed and dug his phone out of the inside pocket. He and Della had switched off their phones shortly after entering the room and had promised to keep them off, and he had kept that promise—at least where his own phone was concerned. Now that their brief interlude was over, he switched it back on. A dozen voice mails awaited him. He ignored them all and went right to his contacts, scrolling through to the one he wanted. A private detective he'd used a number of times, but always only with regard to business. Nevertheless the man had an excellent reputation when it came to investigations of a personal nature, too. Just how excellent, Marcus was about to discover.

He punched the talk button, and after three rings, a voice on the other end answered. Answered with a filthy epithet, but then, that wasn't unexpected considering the source. Or the time of night.

"Damien, it's Marcus Fallon." He gave the other man a few seconds for the synapses in his brain to connect the dots.

"Right," Damien finally said. "Whattaya need?"

"I need your services for something a little different from what I normally hire you for."

"No problem."

"I have a name, a physical description and a former address in New York City. Can you find a person who's now living in Chicago with that?"

"Sure."

"Can you do it soon?"

"Depends."

"On what?" Marcus asked.

"On how bad the person wants to be found."

"How about on how bad *I* want the person found?"

It took another few seconds for more synapses to find their way to the meaning. "How much?" Damien asked.

Marcus relaxed. This was the thing he did best in the world. Well, other than the thing he and Della had spent the weekend doing. He started to turn on the bedside lamp, then remembered he would only see an empty room and changed his mind. "Tell you what," he said, "let's you and I negotiate a deal."

Della had been forced to part with a lot of things in her life. Her family, her friends and her home—such as they were—when she left the old neighborhood at eighteen. Jobs, offices and acquaintances as she'd climbed the professional ladder, moving from one part of Whitworth and Stone to another. An entire new life she'd built for herself in Manhattan. Soon she'd be parting with everything that had become familiar to her in Chicago.

But she didn't think any of those things had been as painful to part with as the crimson velvet Carolina Herrera gown and Dolce & Gabbana shoes, not to mention the Bulgari earrings and pendant and the black silk Valentino opera coat. Not because they were so beautiful and rich and expensive. But because they were the only mementos she had of the time she'd spent with Marcus.

The only physical mementos, at any rate, since she'd left behind the paper on which he'd recorded all of his phone numbers—something for which she was kicking herself now, even if she had memorized all of them. It would have been nice to have something he'd touched, something personal in his own handwriting.

And when had she turned into such a raging sentimentalist? Never in her life had she wanted a personal memento from anyone. Not even Egan Collingwood. That was probably significant, but she refused to think about how.

Besides, it wasn't as though she didn't have

plenty of other reminders of Marcus, she thought as she watched Ava Brenner, the proprietress of Talk of the Town, write out a receipt for the return of the rentals. Della had her memories. Memories that would haunt her for the rest of her life. The way Marcus had traced his fingertips so seductively over the rim of his champagne glass when they were in the club. How his brown eyes had seemed to flash gold when he laughed. The way his jacket had felt and smelled as he draped it over her shoulders. How the snow had sparkled as it had fluttered around him on the terrace and came to rest against his dark hair. The way his voice had rumbled against her ear when he murmured such erotic promises during their lovemaking

But mostly, she would remember the way he looked lying asleep in their bed before she left him.

He'd been lying on his side facing the place where she had been sleeping, his arm thrown across the mattress where she had lain—she'd awoken to find it draped over her. He'd been bathed in a slash of moonlight that tumbled through the window from the clear sky outside. His hair had been tousled from their final coupling, and his expression, for the first time since she met him, had been utterly, absolutely clear. He'd looked…happy. Content. Fulfilled. As if he'd learned the answer to some ancient question that no one else understood.

She'd tried to write him a note, had tried to capture in writing what she so desperately wanted to say to him. But when she'd realized what it was she wanted to say, she'd torn the paper into tiny pieces and let them fall like snowflakes into the tiny handbag that now lay on the counter between her and Ava. They had been silly, anyway, the feelings she'd begun to think she had for him. Impossible, too. Not only because she'd known him less than forty-eight hours. And not only because he was still carrying a torch for someone else. But also because Della wasn't the sort of woman to fall in love. Love was for dreamers and the deluded. And God knew she'd never been either of those.

"There," Ava said as she finished tallying everything. "If you'll sign here that we agree to agree that you returned everything safe and sound, I'll return the full amount of your damage deposit."

"But I'm late getting everything back," Della said. "I was supposed to be here at opening on Sunday. Not Monday."

Ava made a careless gesture with her hand. "I was supposed to be here Sunday, too. But Mother Nature had other ideas for all of us, didn't she?"

Boy, did she ever.

"So Monday morning is the next best thing," Ava continued. "I appreciate you being here so promptly."

Yeah, that was Della. Always perfect timing. Especially when it came to anything that would thoroughly disrupt her life. Had she been five minutes later meeting Egan on New Year's Eve, she would have missed seeing him with the woman she would learn was his wife. Had she been ten minutes later to the office on New Year's Day, she would have missed the memo to her boss that had set everything into motion. She would still be living her life blissfully unaware in New York. Even if she'd ultimately realized Egan was married, and even if she'd quit her job because of him, she would have found another position elsewhere on Wall Street in no time. She would still be picking up her morning coffee at Vijay's kiosk, would still be enjoying Saturdays in Central Park, would still have the occasional night at the Met when she could afford it.

And she never, ever, would have met Marcus.

She couldn't decide if that was a good thing or not. Traditional thinking said it was better to have loved and lost than never to have loved at all, but Della wondered. Maybe it was better to never know what you were missing. Not that she *loved* Marcus. But still…

"Did you enjoy *La Bohème,* Miss Hannan?" Ava asked, bringing Della's thoughts back to the present.

She smiled, only having to fake part of it. "It was wonderful," she said. "I can't remember the last time I enjoyed an evening so much." Or a night afterward, she added to herself. Or a day after that. Or a night after that.

"I've never been to the opera," Ava told her. "Never mind a red-carpet event like opening night. It must have been very exciting, rubbing shoulders with such refined company in a gorgeous setting like the Lyric with everyone dressed in their finest attire."

The announcement surprised Della, though she wasn't sure why. Certainly there were a lot of people out there, especially her age, which Ava seemed to be, who didn't care for opera enough to see it performed live. It was the red-carpet comment and the breathless quality of her voice when she talked about the refined company that didn't gibe. There was an unmistakable air of refinement and wealth about Ava that indicated she must move in the sort of social circle that would promote opera attendance and red-carpet events, never mind gorgeous settings and fine attire.

Both times Della had encountered Ava, the other woman had exuded elegance and good breeding, and had been extremely well put together in the sort of understated attire that only reinforced it. Today, she wore a perfectly tailored taupe suit with pearly buttons, her only jewelry glittering diamond studs in her ears—large enough and sparkly enough for Della to guess they alone cost a fortune. Her dark auburn hair was arranged in a flawless chignon at her nape, and her green eyes reflected both intelligence and sophistication.

Standing across the counter from her, Della was more aware than ever of her impoverished roots. Although she was dressed nicely enough in brown tweed trousers and an ivory cashmere sweater under her dark chocolate trench coat, she felt like more of an impostor than ever. Ava Brenner obviously came from the sort of old money background that Della had had to insinuate herself into—and still never really belonged in. She recognized all the signs, having been surrounded by people like Ava in her job.

Not for the first time, she wondered why the other woman ran a shop like this. She was probably rich enough on her own to do nothing but be idly rich, but she'd been at the boutique late Saturday afternoon when Della picked up her clothes, and she was here bright and early Monday morning, too. For some reason, that made Della glance down at Ava's left hand— no wedding ring. No engagement ring, for that matter. She wondered if Ava had ever loved and lost and how she felt about it.

Della pushed the thought away. Women like Ava could pick and choose whomever they wanted for a mate. She was beautiful, smart, successful and chic. Once she set her sights on a man, he wouldn't stand a chance. He would love her forever and make her the center of his universe. No way would she settle for a one- night stand with a guy she'd never see again.

"Well," Ava said now as she counted out the last of Della's refund, "I hope you'll keep Talk of the Town in mind the next time you need to look your best."

Right. The next time Della would need to look her best would be when she appeared before the grand jury in two weeks. Somehow, though, she was pretty sure one of her suits from her old life would work just fine for that. But maybe in her new life…

She pushed that thought away, too. Her new life would be miles away from Chicago. And there was little chance she'd need to don haute couture for anything in it. It would be nothing but business attire, since she'd be doing little other than establishing herself in a new job, starting all over again from square one. It was going to be a long time before she was earning enough to recapture the sort of life she'd had in New York.

It would be even longer before she trusted any man enough to let him get close to her again.

That hadn't been the case with Marcus, a little voice inside her head piped up. *You got close to him pretty fast. And you trusted him enough to have sex with him.*

But Marcus was different, Della assured the little voice. Marcus had been a one-night stand. It was easy to trust someone you knew you were never going to see again.

Seriously? the voice asked. *Is that the reason you want to go with?*

Um, yeah, Della told the voice.

Fine. But you're only kidding yourself, you know.

Shut up, voice.

"Be careful out there," Ava said, bringing Della's attention back around. "The snow may have stopped, but there are still some slick spots on the sidewalk and slush in the gutters and all kinds of things that could harm you."

Oh, Ava didn't need to tell Della that.

"Don't worry," she said. "I can take care of myself."

And she could, Della knew. She'd been doing it her entire life. That wasn't going to change simply because she had a new life to get under way. Especially since there wouldn't be any Marcuses in her future. Men like him only came along once in a lifetime—if even that often. No way would a man like that show up twice.

In two weeks, Della would be embarking on a second life. A life in which she'd be alone again. Alone still, really, since Egan had never actually been with her the way he could have—should have—been.

Only once in her life had Della really felt as if she was sharing that life—sharing herself—with someone else. And it was someone she would never—could never—see again.

Eight

Nine days after returning the red dress to Talk of the Town, Della was still struggling to go back to her usual routine. It felt like anything but routine now that she had memories of Marcus shouldering their way into her thoughts all the time. The safe house where the feds had placed her was what one would expect to find in middle-class, middle-income, Middle America: sturdy early American furnishings in neutral colors and synthetic fabrics, with white walls and artwork that might have been purchased at any yard sale in suburbia. The lack of personality on the house's part had only contributed to

Della's feelings of entrapment during her time here, but that feeling was compounded in the wake of her separation from Marcus. The handful of days she had left here stretched before her like an oceanful of centuries.

And she was even more fearful now than she'd been before about the uncertainty of her future. Before, she'd been prepared to face life on her own and had felt reasonably certain she would be able to manage. But now she knew what might have been under other, better circumstances. Wonderful. Life with Marcus would have been wonderful. Because he was wonderful. No other man would ever be able to hold a candle to him.

She sighed fitfully. There he was again, at the front of her thoughts. She told herself the only reason she thought him so wonderful was because she knew so little about him. Anyone could be wonderful for thirty-six hours in a small room with no one watching. The time she'd spent with him had been a fantasy. *He'd* been a fantasy. They'd both been playing the role of the phantom, perfect lover. Once free of the hotel room, he might be the same kind of man Egan had turned out to be.

How could she be so certain that Marcus hadn't lied about everything that weekend anyway? He'd said the woman he was waiting for was out of his life, but what if he'd only said that to further his seduction of Della? How could she expect him to have been completely open and honest about himself when she hadn't been open and honest about herself? Once she learned more about him, once she'd discovered what kind of person he really was…

But then, how could she do that when she would never see him again? When she didn't even know his last name? At this rate, he would always be a fantasy to her, and as time went on, he'd grow into an even more legendary lover and all-around great guy, and then she'd really never have a chance to fall in lo—ah, she meant—never have a chance to appreciate someone else she might be compatible with.

A way to counter that possibility came to her immediately, and it wasn't the first time the idea had crept into her brain. This time, it wasn't creeping, though. This time, it was stampeding like a herd of wild, trumpeting wildebeest. And those wildebeest were running right to the laptop in the bedroom.

Maybe she didn't know Marcus's last name. But she knew where he worked. Fallon Brothers. The company must employ thousands of people nationwide, but Marcus wasn't the most common name in the world, and she could narrow the search to Chicago. He'd said himself he was a fixture on a number of websites, so by doing an internet search of his first name and Fallon Brothers and the city of Chicago, she'd probably get a lot of hits. A lot of *notorious* hits. Maybe if she could see him on notorious sites, surrounded by notoriously beautiful women in notoriously compromising situations, she'd realize he wasn't the kind of man she needed in her life anyway. Maybe if she could see him in his natural state of debauchery, it would be easier to forget him.

What could it hurt? She would never see him again. He would never be able to find her, if he was even trying. In a matter of days, she would be swallowed up even deeper into the system

206 CAUGHT IN THE BILLIONAIRE'S EMBRACE

with a new name, address and social security number. And then there would *really* be no way for him to find her.

As she folded herself onto the bed and fired up the laptop, Della's heart began to race, and her stomach erupted with nerves. She wasn't sure what was more exciting—the prospect of learning more about Marcus or the prospect of seeing his face again, even if it was just in an online photo.

She brought up the Google page and clicked on the image option, then typed in the name *Marcus* and the word *Chicago,* along with the words *Fallon Brothers* in quotation marks. And in the blink of an eye—literally—she was staring at the first three rows of what the site told her was hundreds of images. Marcus was in every one of the first batch. And the second, third and fourth batches, too. As she scrolled down the page, she saw him in even more, sometimes alone, but more often with women. Lots of women. Lots of different women. All of them smiling. All of them clinging. All of them beautiful.

Only when Della moved her hand to run her

finger over the mouse pad did she realize it was trembling. In fact, all of her was trembling. She had no idea why. Maybe because seeing Marcus online only reaffirmed that the weekend had really happened. That he really existed. That she had some link, however tenuous, to him. From now on, no matter where she was, or what she was doing, or who she was, she would still be able to find him. She would have physical photographs of him to go along with the insubstantial pictures in her mind. He wouldn't be ephemeral, as she had feared. He could still be with her forever.

Even if he wouldn't be with her forever.

She flexed her fingers to calm them and chose a photo of Marcus alone to move the mouse over. It wasn't one of the candid shots, but rather a posed, formal portrait that must have been one he'd had taken for professional reasons. It was probably from the Fallon Brothers website. When the cursor moved over it, the picture grew larger and added information, starting with a url, then the fact that it was a jpg—sized seventy-something by eighty-seven-something else—then, finally, a description that read Marcus Fallon, Chief Investment Officer, Fallon Brothers Chicago.

Della's hand began to tremble again, and her stomach pitched with nausea.

Marcus Fallon. He was a member of the Fallon family and one of the highest ranking executives in the company. She'd known he must be well-connected to the business. It didn't take seeing him in a place like the Windsor Club to know how well-paid he was or how many perks he must have enjoyed. But this… This went beyond well-connected. And it went way beyond well-paid with excellent perks. He was a descendent of some of the very people who had designed the way the country did business. His ancestors had been the equivalent to royalty in this capitalist society. As such, he was, for all intents and purposes, a prince.

So CinderDella's Prince Charming really was a prince. And she… Well, that would put her in the role of pauper, wouldn't it?

She recalled his assurances that he had friends with clout on the East Coast who might be able to help her out, and her stomach pitched again. Those friends were probably of equal rank to him in New York's financial district. Some of them might very well be officers of Whitworth and Stone. She wouldn't be surprised if some of his friends ended up behind bars because of her. Oh, yeah. He would have loved to help her once he learned what the nature of her "trouble" was. He would have been on the phone in no time flat, tipping off everyone he knew that might be at risk.

Any small hope that Della might have been harboring that she and Marcus still had a chance—and she was surprised to discover she had indeed been entertaining hope, and not such a small amount at that—was well and truly squashed at the realization. Once she gave her testimony to the grand jury, she would be an exile in the financial world. It didn't matter that she was bringing to light illegal activity that should be stopped and punished. No one on Wall Street was going to applaud her, and every door would slam in her face. People like Marcus— and Marcus himself—would want nothing to

210 CAUGHT IN THE BILLIONAIRE'S EMBRACE

do with her. She would be bringing down some very powerful people. And other very powerful people didn't like it when that happened. Especially when it was a peasant doing the tearing down.

Unable to help herself, Della clicked on the link and found herself looking at a larger version of Marcus's photo, and it was indeed on the Fallon Brothers website. She read that he was the eldest great-grandson of one of Fallon Brothers' founding members who would be moving into his father's position as CEO in the not-too-distant future. She read about his hobbies and favorite pastimes—she already knew about opera, squash and port, but the sailing and polo came as something of a surprise—and about his education at the country's finest schools. All in all, it was a sanitized version of the Marcus she knew and wasn't particularly helpful. Once she got past the part about him being the crown prince of the Chicago financial kingdom, she meant.

So she went back to Google and began clicking on some of the other pictures she'd found. There was one of Marcus with a former Miss

Illinois taken at a New Year's Eve party last year. That would have been right around the time Della's world was beginning to fall apart, but Marcus looked as if he didn't have a care in the world. Another photo showed him and a *very* generously endowed redhead at a fundraiser for a children's hospital. Yet another had him sitting on the deck of a high-rise with Lake Michigan in the background and a *very* generously endowed blonde in his lap. The next was a picture of him at some red-carpet event with a woman who looked very much like a certain Hollywood starlet who was known for appearing in public without underwear.

This was how she needed to remember him, Della told herself. In photos taken within months of each other in which he was with a different woman every time. She had to stop thinking of him as Prince Charming and start recognizing the fact that he was just another rich guy with a sense of entitlement who took advantage of everyone who crossed his path. His emotions ran as deep as a strand of hair, and he thought of little other than how to make his own life more enjoyable. He had probably stopped thinking about Della the moment he woke up and found her gone.

He wasn't Prince Charming from a fantastic castle in an enchanted land, she told herself again. He was a big, nasty toad from the toxic swamp of entitlement. The sooner she forgot about him, the better.

She told herself the same thing in a dozen different ways, every time she clicked on a new photograph. But her memories of him crowded out her admonitions. She remembered his smile and his tender touches, and the genuine sadness in his eyes when he had talked about the woman who hadn't been with him that night. That was the real Marcus Fallon, she knew. Maybe not Prince Charming. But not a toad, either.

She just hoped that, wherever he was, he was remembering her fondly, too.

Marcus sat in the study of his Lakeshore Drive penthouse, his black silk robe open over a pair of matching pajama bottoms, nursing a glass of port and sifting through a thin file of information that had been couriered to him that after-noon. Beyond the expansive picture window to his right, Lake Michigan was as inky black as the sky above it, dotted here and there with lights from commercial vessels in the usual shipping lanes that twinkled the same way the stars above them did.

He didn't much notice the vista, however, settled as he was in a boxy, overstuffed club chair that was bathed in the pale amber glow of a floor lamp beside it. Much of the room was amber, in fact, from the coppery fabric of the chair to the golds and browns of the area rug, to the bird's-eye maple paneling to the small, sculpted bronze originals displayed on the built-in shelves. Marcus liked the warm colors. They made him feel calm.

Usually.

Tonight, he felt anything but. Because the file he had thought would be stuffed with informa-tion about Della Louise Hannan of New York City contained little he couldn't have discovered by himself. That didn't, however, make what information was here any less interesting. Especially the part about her having worked at Whitworth and Stone, one of Wall Street's biggest—if not *the* biggest—powerhouses. Marcus knew more than a few people who worked there. And since Della's position as executive assistant to one of its executives would have had her moving in the upper echelon of the business, there was a small chance someone he knew there had at least made her acquaintance. Tomorrow, as soon as the business day started on the East Coast, he would make some phone calls.

Not that having any information about Della's time at Whitworth and Stone would help him much now, since she hadn't worked at the brokerage house for nearly a year. In fact, Della Hannan had pretty much dropped off the face of the map in mid-January of this year and hadn't been seen or heard from since. The apartment where she had lived was now being rented by a married couple who had moved into it in March—and it had been advertised as being a "furnished apartment," because Della had left virtually all of her belongings behind, and her landlord had claimed them on the grounds she hadn't fulfilled the terms of her lease. She'd left her job as abruptly, had simply not come to work one day…or any day afterward.

What was even more troubling was that, in spite of her sudden disappearance, no one had reported her missing. Not a family member, not a friend, not a neighbor, not a lover, not her employer. There was no police report on file, no formal complaint from her landlord, nothing in her personnel file at Whitworth and Stone about why she may have stopped coming to work after more than a decade of not missing a single day.

There was, however, office chatter about why that may have happened. Word in her department was that Della had been dating an executive in another part of the business who had turned out to be married. Whether or not Della had known about his marital status was a bit murky. Either she had known and then been angry that the man refused to leave his wife, or she hadn't known and had left once she discovered the truth. In either event, her office affair seemed to be the reason everyone cited as to why she no longer worked at the company.

It was a reasonable enough explanation. It might even offer a reason for why she had left New York. Except that she was a native New Yorker without family or friends in any other part of the country to whom she might turn for help. Except for the fact that she hadn't started working somewhere else. Except for the fact that there was no record of her having done *any*thing, *any*where, after January 16th. She hadn't applied for any jobs. Hadn't applied for a new driver's license in any state. Hadn't accessed her bank accounts or used her credit cards. Her cell phone service had been canceled due to her failure to pay, in spite of her having had a tidy sum in both a checking and a savings account, neither of which had been touched.

His thoughts halted there for a moment. Her cell phone. He recalled scrolling through her information at the hotel, all the photos and numbers she still had, even though she hadn't called any of them. Obviously she was using a different number now than the one that had been cut off, but why wasn't there a record of her having applied for a new number? Even if she'd requested it be unlisted, his man Damien should have been able to find out what it was. Why hadn't he?

And why had she had all her contacts from the old phone transferred to a new one, clearly wanting to hang on to them even if she wasn't using any of them? He spared a moment to give himself a good mental smack for not bringing up her number on her phone when he'd had it in his hand. Then he cut himself a little slack because he'd been in such a hurry and so pre-occupied by the photos he'd discovered. Still, had he remembered to get her number, it really would have made things a lot easier.

He returned his attention to the P.I.'s report. Marcus might have begun to wonder whether or not the woman he'd met even *was* Della Hannan if it hadn't been for the photographs contained in the file along with the information. He had the picture from her ID badge at Whitworth and Stone, along with copies of photos from her high school yearbook and early driver's licenses. The woman he had met was definitely the same woman in those photos, but, as had been the case with the pictures on her phone, her hair was shorter and darker in all of them.

She'd changed her appearance after she disappeared, but not her name, and his contact hadn't found any evidence that she had any aliases. So there was little chance she was some con artist and a very good chance that everything she had told him about being in trouble was true. The file also had information about Della's early life, which also corroborated what she had told him. There was information about the two brothers she had said she had—one older, one younger. What she hadn't mentioned—probably because she hadn't wanted to dissuade him of his completely wrong ideas—was that she had come from a notoriously bad neighborhood and wasn't the product of wealthy society at all.

At the end of the file was a handwritten note from Damien. It was short and to the point:

The only time someone drops off the face of the planet like this, it's because they're in the hands of the feds. Or else they're trying to avoid the feds and are tapped into a network that makes that happen. I have a friend on the government payroll who owes me a favor. I'll let you know what he finds out.

Marcus lifted his glass to his mouth. But the warm, mellow port did little to soothe the tumultuous thoughts tumbling in his head. So the trouble Della had found herself in in New York was criminal, after all. But which was it with her? Was she helping the authorities or hiding from them?

Who the hell was she? In a lot of ways, she seemed like a stranger to him now. But in another way, she felt even closer than she had been before.

But why and how had she disappeared so completely, not once but twice now? Because she had disappeared again. Damien hadn't been able to find a single clue that might indicate where she was living in Chicago, how long she had been here or when she was planning to leave. Another reason why the man had made the assumption he had in the note, Marcus was certain. Della herself had said she was in trouble. Whether she was helping or hiding, it must be something pretty bad for her to have made herself so invisible.

He closed the file and tipped his glass to his lips again but the glass was empty. He grimaced as he set both the file and the glass on the end table, then rose. He started to walk away, then stopped and went back. For the glass, he told himself. To put it in the dishwasher before he went to bed.

But he picked up the file, too, and opened it again. He took out the photo of Della that had been on her ID badge at Whitworth and Stone. She was the picture of businesslike gravity, unsmiling, wearing no makeup, her short, mannish hair combed back from her face. She looked nothing like she had during the time he'd spent with her. Even after she had washed off her makeup, she had still been beautiful. Even after the inconvenience of the snow, she had still been happy.

And so had he.

That was when Marcus began to understand

his obsession with finding her. Not because she was a mysterious woman in red he couldn't get out of his mind. But because the time he'd spent with her had marked the first time in his life he'd been truly happy. He wasn't sure of the why or when or how of it. He only knew that, with Della, he'd felt different. The same way Charlotte had entered his life when he was a teenager and guided him toward finding contentment with himself, Della had entered his life when he was an adult and guided him toward finding contentment with someone else.

That was what had always been missing before—the sharing. He had shared his life with Charlotte while she was alive, and that had made living it so much better. With Della, he had shared himself. And that made himself so much better. He had been grieving since Charlotte's death, not just for her, but for the emptiness in his life her absence had brought with it. Over the weekend he'd spent with Della, that emptiness had begun to fill again. The hole Charlotte's vacancy had left in his life had begun to close. The wound had begun to heal. With

Della, Marcus had begun to feel again. And the feelings he had…

He started to tuck the photograph into the file, but halted. Instead, after taking his glass to the kitchen, he carried everything into his bedroom. He placed the picture of Della on his dresser, propping it up in front of a lamp there. Even if the woman in the photo didn't look much like the one he remembered, Marcus liked having her in his home. He liked that a lot.

Nine

Two nights after finding Marcus on the internet, Della was still feeling at loose ends about everything that had happened and everything left to come. The media frenzy she had feared would follow the announcement of the arrests at Whitworth and Stone had actually been fairly mild. Geoffrey had told her that wasn't surprising at this point, that when people were that rich and that powerful, it was easy for their attorneys to keep a tight rein on how much information was made available to the press. It would only be after the grand jury arraignment, when evidence was presented to support the charges, thereby making any arguments on the defense's part moot, that the media storm would break. Probably with the fury of a category five hurricane. Geoffrey had also assured her, though, that by the time that happened, Della would be safely ensconced in her new life elsewhere, hidden away from any repercussions.

Hidden away from everything.

But she was doing her best not to think about any of that yet. It was Friday night, the eve of her last weekend in Chicago. On Monday, she would be returning to New York. On Tuesday, she would make her first appearance before the grand jury. In a week, give or take, she would be ushered out of this life and into a new one.

One week. That was all Della Hannan had left. After that…

Oh, boy. She really needed a glass of wine.

She changed into her pajamas, poured herself a glass of pinot noir and grabbed a book that had arrived in that morning's mail. She was settling into a chair in the den when the doorbell of the safe house rang. To say the sound startled her was a bit of an understatement, since she jumped so hard, she knocked over her wine, spilling it over both the book and the snowflake print of her pajama shirt, leaving a ruby-red stain at the center of her chest in its wake.

No one had ever rung the doorbell of the safe house. Not even Geoffrey on those few occasions when he had been here. He always called first to tell her he was coming and at what time, and he gave a couple of quick raps and called out his name once he arrived.

She had no idea who was on the other side of the door now. Not Geoffrey, that was certain. It could be another marshal, or someone from the FBI or SEC who needed to brief her about her grand jury appearance next week. But Geoffrey would have let her know about something like that before he sent anyone over. And no such meeting would ever take place after 10:00 p.m. on a Friday night.

She wasn't sure whether she should sit tight and pretend no one was home, or go to the bedroom for her cell phone to call Geoffrey. Any movement she made might tip-off whoever was outside. Of course, it could just be someone who'd mistaken her address for another on the street. It could be someone delivering a pizza to the wrong house. It could be neighbor kids who thought it would be funny to play a joke on the weird neighbor lady who never left her house. It could be any of those things. It could.

But Della doubted it.

As silently as possible, she closed the book and set it and her half-empty wineglass on the side table, then rose carefully from the chair. The doorbell rang again as she was taking her first step toward the bedroom, setting off explosions of heat in her belly. She went as quickly as she could to the bedroom and grabbed her phone, punching the numbers to Geoffrey's home phone into it but not pushing the send button yet. If it *was* the pizza guy making a mistaken delivery, she didn't want to bother Geoffrey for nothing.

The doorbell rang a third time as she approached the living room, but this time, it was followed by a series of quick, rapid knocks. The front drapes were drawn, as they were every evening, and there were no lights turned on in that room. Della clasped her cell phone tightly in one hand as she came to a halt at the front door, then placed the other hand over the trio of light switches to the left of it. The one closest to her turned on an overly bright bug light on the porch, something that would temporarily blind whoever was out there if she flipped it on. For the moment, however, she only pressed her eye to the peephole to see who was on the other side

Oh, great. A dark, shadowy figure who could be almost anyone. That helped ever so much.

The dark, shadowy figure must have sensed her nearness or heard her approach, however, because as she was drawing back from the peephole, a voice called from the other side, "Della? Are you home? Let me in. We need to talk."

The sound of Marcus's deep voice startled her even more than the doorbell had. Her phone slipped from her fingers and clattered to the floor, her heart began to pound like a marathon runner's and her mind raced in a million different directions. How had he found her? Why was he here? If he'd found her, did someone else know she was here, too? Would his being here compromise the case? Would the feds go so far as to arrest Marcus to keep him under wraps, too?

What should she do?

"Della?" he called out again. "Are you there?"

How *had* he found her? *Why* had he found her? And if he knew her whereabouts, did he know about everything else that had happened, too?

What should she do?

Instead of panicking, however, a strange sort of calm suddenly settled over her, in spite of all the questions, in spite of her confusion, in spite of her fears and misgivings. Even though Della didn't know *what* to do, she knew, very well, what she *wanted* to do….

The chain was latched, as it always was, so, ignoring the phone on the floor, Della turned the three dead bolts on the door and opened it. It was still too dark on the other side for her to make out Marcus clearly, but the absence of light made her feel better. If she couldn't see him, he couldn't see her, either. But it wasn't because of vanity about being in wine-stained pajamas and no makeup or having her hair pulled back in a lopsided ponytail. It was because she knew Marcus couldn't see the real Della Hannan this way. She could still be the fantasy she hoped he remembered her as.

"Della?" he said again, evidently still not certain he'd found her.

All she could manage in response was, "Hi, Marcus."

His entire body seemed to relax at her greeting. "It's really you," he said softly.

The remark didn't invite a response, so Della said nothing. Truly, she had no idea what to say. If Marcus knew she was here, he must know why she was here, too. The marshals had kept her hidden for eleven months without any problems. Yet in less than two weeks, Marcus had managed to find her, without having anything more than her first name. He must know everything about what had happened at this point.

For a long moment, neither of them said a word, and neither moved a muscle. The cold winter wind whipped up behind him, sending his overcoat fluttering about his legs and his hair shuffling around his face. Even though she couldn't make out his features in the darkness, she remembered every elegant contour of his face—the rugged jawline, the patrician nose, the carved cheekbones. As the wind blew past him and against her, it brought his scent, too, the spicy, smoky one she recalled too well. Smelling him again, even one fleeting impression, filled her with desire and hunger and need. It was all she could do not to pull back the chain and throw the door open wide and welcome him into the house, into her life, into her.

But she couldn't do that. She wasn't the woman he thought she was. He might not be the man she'd thought him to be. And even if they could both be what the other wanted, in a matter of days, Della would be disappearing into another life Marcus couldn't be a part of. Her new life would be one into which she was retreating, one that would necessitate living quietly and unob-trusively. His life was one into which he would always go boldly and always live lavishly. And neither the twain could meet.

"Can I come in?" he asked.

"No," she said quickly.

"Della, please. We need to talk."

"We are talking."

"No, we're not. We're greeting each other."

"Then start talking."

He growled out an epithet. "It's cold. Let me in."

Well, he did have a point there, she conceded. Her sock-clad toes were already screaming that they were about to get frostbite. Not to mention her robe was in the other room.

Not to mention she really wanted to see him again. Up close and in good light. She wanted to stand near enough to feel his warmth. Near enough to inhale his scent. And she wanted to pretend again, just for a little while, as she had during their weekend together, that nothing in her life would ever be wrong again.

Unable to help herself, she pushed the door closed enough to unhook the chain, then pulled it open again. Strangely, Marcus didn't barrel immediately through and close it behind himself. Instead, he remained at the threshold, waiting for some cue from her.

Striving to lighten the mood, she said, "Unless

you're a vampire, you don't need a formal invitation."

He hesitated a moment, then said, "I'd like to be invited anyway."

She remembered the night at the club, how he had joined her without asking first, and how he had taken the lead for everything after that. There had been no uncertainty in him that night two weeks ago. But tonight, it was as if he were as uncertain about everything as she was. For some reason, that made her feel a little less uncertain.

"Would you like to come in?" she asked quietly.

He nodded, then took a few steps forward. When she stepped out of the way to let him enter, her foot hit the cell phone on the floor and skittered it to the other side of the foyer. As Della stooped to pick it up, Marcus closed the door behind himself. In the dark room, she could still sense nothing of what he might be feeling or thinking, so she led him into the den. As she walked, she restlessly tugged the rubber band from her ponytail and did her best to fluff and tame her hair at the same time. There was nothing she could do about the wine-spattered pajamas, however, so she only crossed her arms over the stain as best she could and told herself the posture wasn't defensive.

Even if she was feeling a little defensive.

She gestured toward the sofa. "Have a seat," she said as she tucked herself into the chair.

But Marcus didn't sit. Instead, he stood with his hands shoved into his coat pockets, gazing at her.

He looked magnificent, different from the last time she had seen him, but somehow completely unchanged. In person, she'd seen him dressed only in the tuxedo and the bathrobe—one extreme to another—and this incarnation of him was somewhere in between. His trousers were casual and charcoal in color and paired with a bulky black sweater. Coupled with the dark coat and his dark hair, and having come in from the darkness the way he had, he still seemed as overwhelming as he had been the first time she saw him. But his eyes were anxious and smudged with faint purple crescents. His hair was a bit shaggy, and his face wasn't closely shaved. His posture was both too tense and too fatigued, as if he were trapped in some state between the two. Or maybe both conditions had just overwhelmed him. All in all, he looked like a man who had been worrying about something—or perhaps someone—a lot.

When he didn't sit, Della automatically stood again. "Wine?" she asked. Her words were rushed and unsteady as she prattled on. "I just opened a bottle of pinot noir. It's good on a night like this. I'll get you a glass."

Without awaiting a reply, she grabbed her glass and headed into the kitchen to retrieve one for him, her mind racing once again with all the repercussions his arrival into her reality brought with it. Why, oh, why, had she let him in? Why hadn't she called Geoffrey the minute she heard a knock at the door? What if it hadn't been Marcus standing there?

When she turned to go back into the den, she saw him standing framed by the kitchen doorway. He'd removed his coat and ran a hand through his wind-tossed hair, but he didn't look any more settled than she felt. Crumbling under his scrutiny, Della looked away, then, leaving both glasses neglected on the counter, went to the table to fold herself into one of the chairs. Marcus pulled out the chair immediately next to hers and, after sitting down, scooted it in close enough so that his thigh was aligned with her own. For another long moment, neither of them spoke. Neither looked at the other. Neither moved. Finally, unable to stand the silence, Della took the initiative.

"How did you find me?"

He didn't say anything for a minute, only looked down at the table and began to restlessly trace the wood grain with his finger. All he said, though, was, "I'm well-connected."

"No one is that well-connected, Marcus. I've been here for eleven months without anyone knowing. All you had was my first name, and you managed to find me less than two weeks after we—"

She halted when she saw the stain of a blush darkening his cheek. It hadn't been there when he came in, so it couldn't be a result of the cold.

That meant something she'd said had made him uncomfortable. He looked up at her when she stopped talking, then, when he saw her staring at him, his gaze ricocheted away again.

"Marcus, how *did* you find me knowing only my first name?"

Still, he avoided her gaze. "Yeah, about that. I, uh, I actually had more than your first name. I kind of took the liberty of going through your purse while you were in the shower, and I got your last name and your address in New York from your driver's license."

Della closed her eyes at that. How could she have been so careless? She never left the safe house without her driver's license, on the outside chance that if there was an accident of some kind, she could still be returned to the proper authorities. The thought of dying nameless bothered her almost as much as dying friendless. But Della had never expected anyone other than an emergency medical worker or law enforcement officer to see it. She knew enough to use cash instead of her credit cards to keep from being identified, and her phone was one Geoffrey had given her that couldn't be traced. But the personal ID thing…

The fact that she hadn't given it a thought while she was with Marcus was another indication of how much of her trust she had placed in him. Or perhaps misplaced, as the case may be.

"So I had more than your first name to give to…my contact," Marcus confessed.

"The address on my license isn't my address anymore," she told him. "I haven't lived in New York for almost a year."

"I know. But having even your most recent known address along with your full name gave my guy all the information he needed to track you down."

Della let that sink in for a minute. It had been that easy for someone to find her. But no one had. Geoffrey had told Della, too, that all of the defendants had been made aware during questioning and as charges were filed that there was a federal witness in custody who was willing to testify against all of them. And that there were documents this witness had smuggled out that corroborated every charge.

She hadn't slept or eaten much after hearing that, so anxious had she been about whether someone from Whitworth and Stone was trying to track down who the witness was and what information they had, putting together her disappearance with the timing of the investigation.

But no one had. Or, if they did, none had tried to locate her. Or, at least succeeded. Not until Marcus. Who, one would think, didn't have nearly as much at stake. Then she remembered that Marcus was a part of the world she had just punched a big hole in. Who said he wasn't here for the very reason she feared?

No, she immediately told herself. No way. In spite of everything, she still trusted him. In spite of everything, she still…cared for him.

When she trusted her voice again, she asked, "You hired someone to find me?"

"Yes," he acknowledged without hesitation.

"Why?"

This time, his response came less quickly. Finally, he told her, "Because I couldn't stand the thought of never seeing you again."

Something that had been knotted tight inside

Della began to loosen and flow free at his words. Until she remembered how impossible it would be for them to be together.

He started to say something else, but she held up a hand to stop him. "How much do you know about my situation? I mean, if the person you hired to find me found me, he must have uncovered a lot of other information about me, too."

Marcus looked disappointed that she had changed the subject, but he replied, "I know you're in the custody of the U.S. Marshals. I know you're slated to be a material witness for a federal case. Beyond that, I didn't ask for details, except about where you were living now."

She shook her head. "I still can't believe you found me as easily as you did," she said, stalling. "Just what kind of system are the feds running, anyway?"

"It wasn't easy to find you," Marcus countered. "The P.I. I always use to get the information I need can usually get it for me within forty-eight hours."

"Even when it's federally protected?"

"Nothing is foolproof, Della. My guy used to

be a highly placed operative on the government payroll before he went into business for himself. He can find things out others can't because he still has a lot of contacts in high places. In federal, state and city governments."

"He must cost a fortune," she muttered.

"He does."

She spared a moment to find enormous pleasure in the fact that Marcus would spend an exorbitant amount of money to find her, then sobered again when the impact of his discovery settled over her again.

"But even he couldn't work as fast as he usually does," he continued. "And I still didn't get everything I wanted."

She wasn't sure if Marcus was talking only about information in that statement, so she diverted to their original subject. But she did her best to be as vague as possible. She didn't want to say anything that might compromise the hearing next week. She couldn't stand the thought that everything she'd gone through over the last eleven months might end up being for nothing.

But then, without the last eleven months, she

never would have had her weekend with Marcus, would she? So regardless of what did or didn't happen in the future, those tedious, anxious, interminable months could never have been for nothing.

"Look, Marcus, I can't give you any particulars about the case I'm involved in," she said. "I'm not even sure if your mere presence here right now is going to mess everything up or not. Suffice it to say that one day, I was doing my job and living my life and everything was as normal as it could be. The next day, I discovered something my employer was doing that was illegal, and I turned all the information I had over to the proper authorities. The next thing I knew, I was being told I couldn't go back to work, and that I was going to be placed into protective custody while the government took over the investigation. I was told it would only be for a couple of months. That was eleven months ago."

"And to explain your disappearance," Marcus said, "they concocted a story about you having an affair with a married man in another department."

Now it was Della's turn to blush and look away. "That wasn't concocted," she said softly. "And if you know that, then you *do* know something about my situation."

His expression changed then, turning contemplative, and he said nothing for a moment. Then his expression changed once more, this time to one of understanding. "Whitworth and Stone," he said. "That was your employer."

"Yes."

His lips parted fractionally, as if he were going to say something else, then closed again. For another moment, he studied her in silence, then he opened his mouth again. But, again, it took a moment before he spoke. "I read in the trades and the *Wall Street Journal* about the arrests. It was because of you, wasn't it?"

Her stomach knotted again, and she shook her head vehemently. "I can't say anything about it."

"You don't have to," he told her. "It didn't occur to me until now to put it all together. There just hasn't been that much in the news about what's really going on there. There was so little fanfare, in fact, that most of us figured the charges were bogus, just the government flexing its muscle to keep Wall Street in its place, or that it would turn out with one or two guys getting a slap on the wrist for some minor infractions. It never occurred to me that they'd actually make a federal case out of it."

Della said nothing, but couldn't pull her gaze away from his. The wheels were clearly spinning in his brain now, and he was obviously able to put way more than two and two together. A man like him, as highly placed as he was in the financial community, could fully appreciate how much was at stake here, and how much trouble a company like Whitworth and Stone could be in. A man like him would know exactly how important Della's role was in what was happening, and he would understand completely how devastating her impact would be.

He nodded slowly. "But the reason there hasn't been much media coverage is precisely because of how massive a case this is going to be. Executives that high up, with that much money and that many resources at their disposal—not to mention that much to lose—can afford the kind of lawyers who can keep things quiet, at least for a while."

Still, Della said nothing. Still, she couldn't look away.

"It never occurred to me to put those arrests together with your disappearance," Marcus said. "The married lover story made a lot more sense."

"I didn't know he was married," she said, finally relieved to be able to talk about something that wouldn't compromise the case. "I was supposed to meet him on New Year's Eve. Though after midnight because he said he had a professional dinner to attend. I arrived a little early and saw him kissing another woman good night before putting her into a cab. When I asked who she was, he informed me she was his wife, who he had no intention of leaving because, by the way, he also had three kids and his wife's family was so well-connected socially and financially, and he couldn't afford to lose those connections."

Marcus's expression then indicated the wheels were still turning in his head, though they might be going in a different direction now. "You disappeared in mid-January, meaning you must have uncovered the wrongdoing at Whitworth and Stone right before that."

"On New Year's Day," she said without thinking. But that wasn't compromising information, was it? Surely not.

Marcus nodded slowly, as if making more connections. "So you found out on New Year's Eve that the man you were seeing was married, and then, hours later, discovered that your employer was involved in matters that threatened national security."

"That's it in a nutshell, yeah."

"Sucky way to start the new year."

She wished she could laugh, then wondered if she would ever be able to find humor in anything again. "Yeah."

"You know, anyone else would have been devastated by either one of those things, but even after suffering both, you still had the presence of mind, and the courage, to do the right thing."

Della had never really looked at it like that. "I just did what anyone else in that position would do."

"No, you didn't," he said. "A lot of people would have walked away from both and wallowed in self-pity. Or they would have kept their mouths shut and not risked losing their job or their benefits or anything else that might mess up their life."

"Maybe…"

"Instead, you risked everything to make sure the people who were putting other people—strangers you didn't even know—in danger didn't get away with what they were doing."

"Yes."

He lifted a hand and started to reach for her, then hesitated, as if fearing how she would react. Reluctantly, without touching her, he dropped his hand to the table. "And you have to ask why I came looking for you."

Whatever was left of the knot inside her unraveled. In spite of that, she told him, "You shouldn't have come, Marcus."

"Why not?"

"Because I'm leaving Chicago in three days, and I'm not coming back."

"I know that was your plan before, but now—"

"Now, it's still the plan," she told him. "I can't stay here, Marcus."

"Why not?"

How did she say this without having it sound melodramatic and paranoid? Probably, she should simply spell it out. "Because after I give my testimony to the grand jury, I'm going to be one of the most hated people on Wall Street. No one's going to give me a job. The people I'm going to help put away have contacts every-where. Not only in other brokerage houses, but in banks and all kinds of businesses. They have corporate America eating out of their hands. No one will hire me. Whistle-blowers might make for great movies and documentaries, but in the real world, their lives are shattered. They can't find work. They can't support their families. They lose everything."

He was still looking at her in a way that made clear he didn't understand what she was saying. So Della spelled it out further. "After this thing is over, the government is giving me a new ID. New name, new social security number, new history, new everything. They're going to move me someplace where I have a chance to start over again where no one will know me, and where there's no chance I'll be recognized. I'll be able to find a job doing something I love, something I'm good at. I won't be Della Hannan anymore."

Marcus sat back in his chair and inspected her openly now. "Then who will you be? Where will you go?"

"I don't know yet," she said. "But it won't be here."

"Why not here? It's as easy to start over in Chicago as anywhere else. Better. There's a vital financial community here. Where else are you going to go and find that? Go ahead and change your name and history. You'll still be Della. You'll still be the woman I met at Palumbo's. You'll still be the woman I spent the most amazing weekend of my life with. You'll still be the woman I—"

He halted before finishing, probably because Della had started shaking her head as soon as he finished his first sentence. "If I stay here, Marcus, I'll want to be with you."

He gaped at her. "And that's a problem?"

"Yes!" she cried. "Because you're so…" She recalled the adjective he'd used himself. "Notorious. You're all over the society pages and a regular fixture on a lot of celebrity websites. You said so yourself."

Now he closed his mouth. She was pretty sure he was starting to understand. But since she was still in spell-it-out mode, Della continued, "You live a big life, Marcus. It's what makes you happy. It's who you are. You like your notoriety. And I don't blame you," she hastened to add. "Big life suits you. You were born for the spotlight. But me…" She shrugged lightly. "I wasn't born for a big life. And now, more than ever, I need to be invisible. It's the only way I'll be able to rebuild my life. It's the only way I'll be able to get back everything I've lost."

"In other words, you don't want to be seen with me."

"I *can't* be seen with you," she corrected him. "What if someone recognizes me? What if, as I'm starting to get my groove back, someone in your world realizes who I really am? They could destroy everything I have." She swallowed hard against the anguish she felt threatening. "And they could hurt you, too. Doing what you do for a living, if you were seen consorting with the woman who brought down Whitworth and Stone, no one would ever trust you again. Then your life would be shattered, too. I can't let that happen to you. I can't be responsible for it."

"I'd never worry about something like that," he told her.

"I would always worry about it," she said. "It would never work out for us, Marcus," she said. "It would be a mistake for me to stay. That is just as well, because after Monday, I'll be gone."

He leaned forward in his chair, taking both of her hands in his. "No, Della, you can't. We need to talk more about—"

This time, when Marcus stopped speaking, it wasn't because he cut himself off. This time, it was because of a loud crash in the living room—which Della was pretty sure was the sound of the front door being broken in—followed by a wildly shouted, "Della, it's Geoffrey! Are you okay?"

And then, just like in the movies, everything turned to chaos.

Ten

Marcus sat on the sofa in Della's house—even though both obviously really belonged to Uncle Sam—and wondered when his life had morphed into a Quentin Tarantino film. One minute, he'd been sitting at the kitchen table trying to tell her how he felt about her, and the next, he had been face down on the linoleum with some guy's knee in the small of his back yelling that he should keep his hands where the guy could see them at all times.

At least the guy, whom Della had eventually been able to introduce as the federal marshal assigned to keep an eye on her, had taken off the handcuffs after shoving Marcus onto the sofa. Now, as he rubbed at his wrists and tried to crane his head around the man to see how Della was faring, the guy—who Marcus couldn't help thinking looked like an older version of Dwight Schrute, only not as well-dressed—leaned the same way he was trying to look, cutting off his view of Della. Again.

"Geoffrey, it's okay," Della said. Again.

Marcus had gathered from the frantic exchange between Della and the marshal only moments ago that before answering her front door, she had dialed Geoffrey's number without pressing the call button, and that when she dropped the phone on the floor, it had somehow performed that function anyway. Geoffrey had answered his phone after seeing Della's name attached to the caller ID and heard her talking to someone in the distance. Even though the conversation hadn't sounded threatening and she hadn't sound frightened, she wasn't supposed to be talking to *anyone,* so he had leaped into action and driven to the safe house to check on her. Then, when he mistook the wine stain on her shirt for blood…

Well, that was when the knee in Marcus's back had nearly broken his spine.

Now, however, all was well. The marshal was only looking at him as if he planned to cap him in both kneecaps with the sidearm he hadn't even had the decency to reholster. At least he wasn't pointing the weapon at Marcus anymore.

"Tell me one more time," Geoffrey said, "what the hell you think you're doing here."

Marcus had already told him that twice—as had Della—but Geoffrey didn't seem satisfied. This, okay, maybe Marcus could understand, since he hadn't been completely honest with the guy. But there was no way he was going to tell a total stranger he was here because he was in love with Della Hannan when he hadn't even told Della that yet.

"He's a friend," Della said. Again.

Marcus looked at Geoffrey to see if that would satisfy him. It clearly did not.

"I thought you didn't have any friends in Chicago," Geoffrey told Della. Still looking at Marcus.

When Della didn't reply right away, the marshal glanced over his shoulder in silent inquiry, then quickly returned his attention to Marcus. As if realizing his dilemma in not being able to see them both at the same time, Della moved to sit on the sofa, too. Marcus tried not to read too much into the fact that she crowded herself into the corner as far from him as she could get. But—call him an alarmist—the gesture wasn't exactly encouraging.

Della glanced at Geoffrey, then back at the floor, looking like a twelve-year-old who'd been caught with her first cigarette. "I met him two weeks ago," she said.

Geoffrey narrowed his eyes at her. "How could you have met him two weeks ago when you never leave the house?"

Della nibbled her lip nervously but said nothing.

"Della?" Geoffrey prodded.

"Yeah, about that," she said. She then launched into a long, winding, somewhat convoluted explanation about sneaking out of the safe house from time to time due to extreme cabin fever, then about some promise she'd made to herself as a child, then she spoke at length about opera in general and *La Bohème* in particular, then she backtracked to something about a little shop off Michigan Avenue and haute couture, then she moved on to dinner, then Marcus, and then—

And then she stopped abruptly. Probably, Marcus thought, because she'd gotten to the part about where the two of them checked into the Ambassador Hotel.

At that point, had Geoffrey been a character in an old-time novel, he was what would have been referred to as *apoplectic.* But his voice was level when he told Della, "I cannot believe you've been sneaking out of the house on a regular basis without letting me know where you were going."

"Only a few times," she said defensively. When she looked up and saw how sternly her caretaker was eyeing her, she amended, "Okay, six. But that's all. And if I'd told you, you wouldn't have let me go. I was always careful."

Geoffrey spent a few more minutes admonishing her like a child and making her look even guiltier, but there was little he said that Della— or Marcus—could take exception to.

That didn't, however, stop Marcus from taking exception. "Give it a rest, Geoffrey," he interrupted the man midsentence. "It's the feds' fault for keeping her cooped up here for eleven months."

Both Geoffrey and Della glared at him for that. Geoffrey's irritation Marcus could understand, but Della's?

"Don't make this worse than it already is," she told him. "Geoffrey's right. I shouldn't have left the safe house. Ever."

Something in the way she said it made Marcus think her reasoning had less to do with the fact that she'd broken the rules and more to do with the repercussions of her actions. He just hoped one of the repercussions in question wasn't having met—and spending a weekend with—him.

He opened his mouth to try and reassure her that the weekend the two of them had spent together had been anything but wrong, but Geoffrey jingled the handcuffs he was still holding and said, "Keep it up, Fallon, and you're going to find yourself in federal custody, too. Only it won't be a safe house you'll be going to."

Yeah, yeah, yeah, Marcus wanted to say. He knew his rights when it came to law enforcement. He watched network television.

"I only meant—"

"I don't care what you meant," Geoffrey admonished. "I really ought to take you into custody, at least until Della leaves town."

"But—"

"But since she'll vouch for you, and since, like she said, you're such a paragon of professionalism and a scion of the community—" there was no mistaking the sarcasm in his voice when he said that last part "—I'm going to let you go."

Marcus bit back the indignation he felt and forced himself to mutter a reasonably tempered, "Thank you."

"But you'll have to leave the premises now and not come back."

Okay, so much for the reasonable temper. "What? But you just said yourself that Della vouched for me, so what's the harm in—"

"I don't have to explain the harm again," Geoffrey stated emphatically. Then, to hammer it home, he added, "To either of you. Now maybe the physical threat to Della is minimal, but she's got a big job to do next week, and we can't have it messed up because she gets a little stir-crazy being cooped up."

Both Marcus and Della started to speak at once, but Geoffrey lifted a hand to stop them. When neither of them stopped, the marshal raised his voice louder than theirs and talked right over them.

"Here's what's going to happen," he said. "Fallon, you're going to go home and forget you ever saw Della Hannan here in Chicago."

"Oh, no I'm not," Marcus said. He didn't care how loud the other guy was talking.

"Yes. You are," Geoffrey countered. "And, Della." He turned his attention to her before Marcus had a chance to object again. "You're going to pack everything you brought with you to Chicago while I wait."

"What? But why?" Della sounded as annoyed as Marcus was.

"Because you're checking out of Chez Uncle

Sam tonight," Geoffrey told her. "The safe house has been compromised. You can't stay here."

"But Marcus is the only one who knows—"

"The safe house has been compromised," Geoffrey repeated. "You can't stay here. Now go pack your bags. We'll find you somewhere else to stay for the next couple of nights—not that you're going to be let out of my sight, meaning I'll be missing my favorite nephew's bar mitzvah on Sunday, thank you very much—and then, Monday, you'll fly back to New York as scheduled."

For a moment, Marcus thought Della was going to fight the other man's edict. Her back went ramrod-straight, her eyes flashed with anger and her hands doubled into fists. Then, as quickly, her entire posture changed. Her shoulders rolled forward, her gaze dropped to the floor, her fingers uncurled.

"All right," she conceded softly. "I guess it's inevitable."

"And, Della," Geoffrey said, bringing her attention to him. "I want the cell phone that we gave you. You're not to have any contact with the outside world until after the grand jury hearing. And you're going to be assigned a twenty-four-hour escort in New York—no, *two* twenty-four-hour escorts in New York," he hastily corrected himself, "until the powers that be say it's okay to cut you loose into the program."

"The program?" Marcus asked.

Now Geoffrey turned to look at him. "WITSEC," he said. "The Witness Security Program. You might know it better as witness protection, thanks to our good buddies in Hollywood," he added with more sarcasm.

Marcus looked at Della. "Is that true?" he said.

She continued to study the floor as she replied. "Yes."

"You're going into the witness protection program?"

"I told you I had to start over somewhere new, Marcus, where no one would know me. Where I had a whole new identity."

"I know, but I thought…"

Now she did look at him. "You thought what?"

He struggled over his words. "I thought…I mean, I just figured… After everything that happened between you and me…" He halted, took a deep breath and released it slowly. "Witness protection means you'll never be able to contact anyone from your old life," he finally said. "It means I won't have any way to find you. Not even my guy with the contacts could find you there."

"What guy with the contacts?" Geoffrey asked, turning suspicious again.

Marcus ignored him. Della still looked at the floor.

"Della," he pleaded. "Don't do it."

"What guy with the contacts?" Geoffrey repeated. "If he knows how to get past government smoke-screens, we need to know about him."

"Then you can question me at home later." Marcus ground out the words without sparing the marshal a glance.

"Oh, we will, Mr. Fallon. We will."

Della remained silent.

Marcus knew there was no way he would be able to find her once she disappeared. It was obvious that Geoffrey's concern for her went beyond what a federal marshal would undertake.

From the moment he'd crashed into the kitchen, there had been an unmistakable air of paternity about the guy. He was protecting Della the way he would protect a daughter. Marcus might as well be doing battle with a mama polar bear.

"Della," he said again, "please. You and I need to talk."

"Not tonight, you won't," Geoffrey assured him. Then, to Della, in a much gentler voice, he said, "Go pack your stuff. I'll call around and find another place for you. A place that's *safe*," he said, looking back at Marcus, still obviously not trusting him.

Della lifted her head and looked at Marcus, her eyes brimming with tears. "I'm sorry," she told him. "I—I just…I can't—" She shook her head. "Goodbye, Marcus."

And then she was off the sofa and disappearing into the hallway. Unthinkingly, Marcus stood to follow her, but a heavy hand on his shoulder stopped him.

"Front door's that way," Geoffrey told him. "Use it."

Marcus didn't have much choice but to obey.

He took two broad steps in that direction, but stopped to look down the hall. There was a light on in one of the bedrooms at the end, and he could see Della's shadow moving around in front of the lamplight. That was all she was to him now—a shadow. Just as he'd been before she came into his life, Marcus was back to being alone.

No, wait, he realized as the thought formed in his head. It wasn't like before at all. Because before, Marcus hadn't realized what he was missing. Before, he hadn't recognized the emptiness, because he'd been able to fill it with mind-numbing carousing and willing, if faceless, women. Before, Marcus had been able to delude himself that he had everything he could possibly ever want and that his life lacked absolutely nothing. Before, he had been able to pretend that he was happy and contented. But now…

Now he really did know what happiness and contentment were. Because those were the things he'd felt when he was with Della. Now he knew how full, how fun, how fantastic his life could be. Now he understood how much more enjoyable it was to share life with someone else. He realized that loving someone wasn't just something a person *did,* but how being in love was something a person *was.* Marcus was in love with Della, and that completed him as a human being. It was something that brought him greater joy, greater peace, than he ever could have imagined. With Della gone…

Well. He would still be in love with her. He would always be in love with her. But with her gone, so went a part of himself. A part she would always keep with her, but a part he would never have back. Not unless he had Della.

And Della would be someplace where the feds would make sure she was never found again.

Although the grand jury hearings lasted less than a week, they seemed even more interminable and emotionally draining than the eleven months Della had spent cooped up in Chicago. Because she was the only witness the federal prosecutors had, her testimony took up the majority of the time, and she spoke for hours every day, until she thought she would run out of voice and words and nerve. By the end of the proceedings, all she wanted was to escape into her new life where she would be left alone.

Until she remembered that being alone would mean, well, being alone. If only she could take Marcus with her…

But she couldn't do that. What made things more difficult was that, even after the grand jury hearing concluded, she still wouldn't be left alone—not yet. At some point, she would have to return to New York to repeat everything she'd said. Because the grand jury had been given an overwhelming amount of evidence against Whitworth and Stone and a number of its highest-placed executives. They would, without question, rule that the case go to trial. A trial that would involve the same star witness—her. Only then would she be able to slip back into her new anonymity. Only that time, it *would* be forever.

For some reason, the word *forever* made her think about Marcus. But then, nearly everything made her think about Marcus. Every time someone brought her a cup of coffee, she thought about him pouring one for her in the hotel. Whenever room service showed up with her dinner at the hotel where she was staying in New York, she thought of how Marcus had ordered such a breakfast feast for her. When she looked out over all the power suits in the court-room, she thought of him. When she saw men in long overcoats on the streets of New York, she thought of him.

But worst of all, Friday evening, as she left the federal courthouse in New York City, dressed for the weather in a camel-hair coat and red scarf, mittens and hat, with an equally bundled-up marshal on each side of her, it started to snow. Maybe not as furiously as it had the night she met Marcus in Chicago, but seeing the spar-kling white snowflakes tumbling out of the inky sky, Della was overwhelmed by memories of what had happened on the terrace of the Wind-sor Club, when she'd had the most incredible sexual experience of her life with a mysterious lover named Marcus.

Though he hadn't been a mystery for long.

Della had gotten to know him pretty well during their time together, even better than she had realized. Over the time that had passed since their weekend together—and even more since they'd parted ways in Chicago—she had come to understand exactly how very well she did know Marcus, and how very deeply she'd come to feel for him. She couldn't pinpoint the moment when it had happened during their weekend together—maybe when he was wiping away her tears or pouring her a cup of coffee or tracing a finger lovingly over her naked shoulder—but she had fallen in love with Marcus. What had started as a sexual response had grown in mere hours to an emotional bond. She only wished she had admitted that to herself when she still had the chance to tell him.

She loved Marcus. Maybe she hadn't admitted it to herself at the time because the feeling was so new and unfamiliar to her. But it was that newness and unfamiliarity that finally made her realize she was in love. Being with Marcus had made her feel complete for the first time in her life. When she was with him, she'd felt as if she could handle anything. Everything that had been wrong in her life had suddenly seemed less likely to overtake her. She'd been less fearful when she was with Marcus. Less anxious. Less troubled. But most of all, with Marcus, she'd been happy. Since leaving him…

Since leaving him, nothing felt right. Even the snow falling down around her now didn't have the magic for her it would have had—that it did have—only a few weeks ago.

"Stop," she said to the two marshals as she paused halfway down the courthouse steps.

The man on her right, whose name was Willoughby, halted in his tracks, but the woman on her left, Carson, continued down two more steps, glancing right, then left, before turning to face Della.

"What's wrong?" Carson asked.

"Nothing. I just… It's snowing," she finally said, as if that should explain everything.

"So?"

"So I want to stand here for a minute and enjoy it." *Or at least try to.*

She heard Willoughby expel an irritated sigh,

saw Carson roll her eyes. Della didn't care. She'd done a lot for her country this week. She'd sacrificed the past year of her life. The least her country could do was let her enjoy a minute in the snow.

She closed her eyes and tipped her head back, letting the icy flakes collect on her bare cheeks, nose and mouth. She sighed as she felt them melt one by one, only to be replaced by others. She heard the sound of a honking taxi, felt the bustle of people around her, inhaled the aroma of a passing bus. And she smiled. She loved the city. She didn't care what anyone said about noise and crowds and traffic. All those things only proved how alive the city was. She had grown up in this place. It was a part of her. No matter how badly it had treated her—as a child or as an adult—she couldn't imagine living anywhere else. She hoped, wherever her new life was, she would live in a big city again. Because maybe, just maybe, being surrounded by people—even if they were strangers—would help keep the loneliness at bay.

"Della."

Her eyes flew open at the sound of the familiar voice. The first thing she saw was Carson's back, because the woman had stepped in front of her. The second thing she saw was how Willoughby was reaching inside his open overcoat for what she knew would be a weapon. The third thing she saw was Marcus.

At first, she thought she was imagining him, because he looked so much as he had that night at the Windsor Club, dark and handsome and mysterious, surrounded by swirls of snow. The only difference was that he'd exchanged the tuxedo for a dark suit. That and the fact that he looked so very lost and alone.

"Marcus," she said softly. She covered Carson's shoulder with one hand as she curled the fingers of the other over Willoughby's arm. "It's okay," she told them both. "He's…a friend."

Carson didn't even turn around as she said, "Our orders, Ms. Hannan, are to—"

"I'll take full responsibility for anything that happens," Della said.

"That's not the problem," Carson told her. "The problem is—"

But Della didn't wait for her to finish. She strode away from the two marshals, down the steps of the courthouse, until she stood on the one above Marcus, facing him. It was only then that she realized he was holding a suitcase. He must have come here straight from the airport. He must have been following the court proceedings and knew that by today, they'd come to an end.

"Hi," she said softly.

"Hi," he replied just as quietly.

Neither of them said anything more for a moment. Marcus set his suitcase on the ground beside him and shoved his hands deep into his overcoat pockets. So Della took the initiative, raised her mittened hands to his shoulders, leaned forward and covered his mouth with hers. She told herself it was because she hadn't had a chance to kiss him goodbye. Not at the hotel, and not at the safe house. So this was what that would be. A chance to tell him goodbye properly.

Funny, though, how the moment her lips met his, it didn't feel like goodbye at all. Because the next thing she knew, Marcus was roping his arms around her waist and crushing her body against his, pulling her completely off the concrete. What had been frigid air surrounding her suddenly turned blistering, and heat exploded at her center, igniting every extremity. The memories of him that had tortured her all week evaporated, replaced by the impressions of his reality. She felt his arms around her waist again, the scruff of his beard against her cheek again, the solid strength of his shoulders beneath her hands again. She couldn't believe he was actually here.

Wait a minute. What was he doing here?

The thought made her pull away from him, but Marcus followed and captured her mouth with his again. Although he set her down on the step, he curved his hands over her hips to keep her there and kissed her more deeply still. She allowed herself to get lost in blissful sensations for another long moment. But when she heard the sound of not one, but two throats clearing not so indiscreetly behind her, she found the wherewithal to pull away from him again.

Marcus must have heard the marshals' reactions, too, because he didn't try to reclaim Della this time. He did, however, move to the same step she was on and loop an arm around her shoulders, then he pulled her close, as if he were afraid her guardians would try to take her from him again.

But neither marshal seemed eager to come between them. In fact, they were both smiling.

"He looks like more than...a friend," Carson said.

"Yeah, I don't have any...friends...like that," Willoughby agreed. "I don't think my wife would like it too much if I did."

Della felt Marcus relax beside her. But he still didn't loosen his hold on her. Not that she cared.

"Do you mind?" Della said to the two marshals. "Can I have a few minutes to talk to my... friend?"

Carson and Willoughby exchanged a wary look, then turned back to Della.

"I'm sorry, Ms. Hannan," Carson said, "but privacy is one thing a federal witness doesn't get much of. And you're not out of protective custody yet. If you want to talk to your...friend...

it's going to have to be in front of me and Willoughby."

"It's okay, Della," Marcus said.

With one more pleading look aimed at her escorts—who both regretfully shook their heads
in response—she turned to Marcus. He lifted a
hand to her face to trace the line of her cheek-
bone, her nose, her jaw and her mouth. He didn't
seem to be bothered by their audience. Then
again, Della was so happy to see him, she didn't
really care who saw them, either.

"I'm going to have to get used to this witness
security thing sooner or later, anyway," Marcus
said. "It might as well be now."

The remark puzzled her. "Why do you have
to get used to it?"

He inhaled a deep breath and released it slowly,
then dropped his hand from her face so that
he could take her hand in his. When her mittens hindered his efforts, he gently tugged one
off. Then he wove their fingers together and
squeezed tight.

"I have to get used to it," he said, "because I'm
going with you."

Her mouth fell open a bit at that. "What are you talking about?"

"I'm going with you."

She shook her head. "Marcus, that's crazy talk. You don't know what you're saying."

"I know exactly what I'm saying." He lifted her hand to his mouth and pressed a small kiss in the center of her palm. Then he said a third time, "I'm going with you."

"But you can't," she insisted. "You have a life in Chicago. A big life. A larger-than-life life. There are lots of people who will miss you if you disappear."

"None that matters as much as you," he told her.

"But your friends—"

"—are not particularly close ones," he finished for her. "They don't matter as much as you."

"Your family—"

"—is more of a corporate entity than a family," he assured her. "I've spent ninety percent of my life rebelling against them and the other ten percent taking advantage of them. We're not that close, either. They definitely don't matter as much as you."

"But your business. Your job is—"

"—mostly as a figurehead," he told her. "It especially doesn't matter as much as you." He gave her hand another gentle squeeze. "I don't do that much for Fallon Brothers as it is now, Della. Once I'm in charge, I'll do even less. I'll just make a lot more money for that lack of performance. Corporate America is kind of funny that way."

She latched on to the money thing. "Your money. You can't walk away from all that. It's—"

"—money," he concluded easily. "That's all. Just money. It doesn't even come close to mattering as much as you."

"That's all?" she echoed incredulously. "Marcus, that's a lot of money you're talking about. Millions of dollars."

He only smiled, tugged off her other mitten and took that hand in his, too, giving it a kiss identical to the other one. "Billions, actually," he said matter-of-factly.

All Della could manage in response to that was a soft squeak.

That only made Marcus laugh. "Della. I would think you, of all people, would understand how that much money can bring *a lot* of trouble into a person's life. It's not that hard to walk away from it."

"Oh, right," she sputtered. "Spoken like someone who's never had to go without money in his life."

"Della, there's more to life than money," he stated unequivocally. "The best things in life are free. Simple pleasures are the best. Money is the root of all evil."

She shook her head at him, but couldn't help smiling. Probably because of the warm, gooey sensations meandering through her. "When did you open an unlimited account at Platitudes 'R' Us?" she asked.

"Actually," he said lightly, "the account is at words-to-live-by-dot-com. But you're right—it is an unlimited one." He leaned in close, moving his mouth to her ear. Very quietly, he whispered, "Besides, the woman I intend to spend the rest of my life with is adamant about rebuilding her career. She can take care of me. She loves me to distraction, after all."

The warm gooeyness inside her swirled into a river of sweet, sticky goodness. Unable to help herself, Della leaned forward to press her forehead against Marcus's shoulder. He looped his arms around her waist and settled his chin on the crown of her head.

"See there?" he said softly. "You do love me, don't you?"

She was amazed to hear an unmistakable uncertainty in his voice. "Yes," she whispered against the fabric of his coat.

Now he pressed a kiss to the crown of her head. "Good. Because I love you, too."

He loved her, too, Della thought. He loved her, too. He loved her, too. It was like a magic incantation in her brain, breaking all the evil spells of her old life and bestowing new ones in their wake. He loved her, too. He loved her, too.

"But, Marcus," she said softly, "there's so much more you should consider besides—"

"Della, there's *nothing* more to consider than

you. I've had weeks to think about you and me, and you know what I figured out that was most significant?"

With her head still pressed against his chest—it felt so good to have it there—she asked, "What?"

"What was significant was that I didn't need weeks to think about it. I didn't even need days to think about it. I didn't need to think at all. I only needed to feel. And what I feel for you, Della..."

When he didn't finish, she tilted her head back to look at him. He was still smiling, but there was something in this one she hadn't seen in any of the others before. Peace. Contentment. Happiness. She recognized it, because with him here beside her, she felt all those things, too.

"What I feel for you is like nothing I've felt before in my life. And I like it, Della. I like it a lot. I want to feel this way forever." He dipped his head to hers and kissed her again. When he pulled back, he repeated resolutely, "So I'm coming with you."

Della didn't know why she kept wanting to

object, but she couldn't quite keep herself from giving it one more shot. "But what if—"

Marcus lifted his hand to press his fingers lightly against her mouth. "It doesn't matter what if," he said. "Whatever happens, Della, we'll face it together. We'll *be* together. That's all that matters."

"But—"

"Shh," he said.

And then he dropped his fingers from her mouth to place a chaste kiss there instead. It was enough to quiet her voice if not quell her reservations. He was right, she told herself. It didn't matter what the future brought, as long as the two of them were together. She'd brought herself up from very humble beginnings and made a decent life for herself before everything went wrong at Whitworth and Stone. And she'd managed to make the best of a bad situation for eleven months in Chicago. The place from which she would be starting over again now was infinitely better than the places where she'd started off before. And this time, she wouldn't be embarking on the journey alone. This time, she would be with Marcus. And that made even the bleakest prospects tolerable.

He tucked a strand of dark blond hair behind her ear and leaned down until his mouth hovered just next to it. His warm breath on her cold skin sent a delicious shiver down her spine. Or maybe it was his simple nearness that did that. As he had with her mouth, he placed a small, soft kiss on her ear lobe. Then he pulled back far enough to murmur in a voice too soft for anyone but her to hear, "Besides. Thirty percent of my wealth is liquid and highly accessible. It's in conveniently numbered Swiss bank accounts, and I'll be able to get to it whenever I want. We won't starve, sweetheart. Trust me."

Meaning, she thought with a grin, that she would never have to settle for rented clothing again. A single, genuinely happy chuckle escaped her. But even this information didn't matter. It was as Marcus said, all that mattered was that the two of them would be together. Forever.

She looked at the suitcase by his feet. It was the size of one that could be carried onto a plane. There wasn't much that would fit in a bag that size.

"That's all you're bringing with you into our new life?" she asked.

He glanced down at the bag, then back at Della. "It's more than I need, really. Because everything I need is right here."

And then he kissed her again. And kissed her. And kissed her. And kissed her. In fact, he kissed her so long, and so many times, that only the appearance of Carson and Willoughby on each side of them made him stop. Even at that, it took a moment for Della to remember her surroundings. But when she saw the two marshals smiling at her, she remembered all too well.

She'd completed what she'd come to New York to do. Now it was time to head into a new chapter of her life.

"Carson, Willoughby," she said to the two marshals. "Tell your boss there's been a slight change in my plan." She turned to Marcus and looped her arm through his. "Tell her I'm going to have one more piece of baggage than I'd planned."

And as baggage went, she thought, Marcus was the kind she would happily carry with her forever.

* * * * *